"I haven't come here to exchange pleasantries, Miss Tyrell."

Jon continued. "And I warn you now that you'll be wasting your time trying to play off your tricks. My taste has never run to overendowed blondes, and even if it did, I'm a bit too awake to the time of day to be taken in by a cheap little gold digger like you."

"How dare you speak to me like that?" Lacey protested.

Again that indifferent regard swept down over her. "I knew what you were before I came here, and nothing I've seen so far would make me revise that opinion," he asserted with cool derision.

SUSANNE McCARTHY grew up in South London but she always wanted to live in the country, and shortly after her marriage she moved to Shropshire, England, with her husband. They live with lots of dogs and cats in a house on a hill. She loves to travel—but she loves to come home. As well as her writing, she still enjoys her career as a teacher in adult education, though she only works part-time now.

Books by Susanne McCarthy

SUSANNE McCARTHY

No Place for Love

Harlequin Books

TORONTO • NEW YORK • LONDON
AMSTERDAM • PARIS • SYDNEY • HAMBURG
STOCKHOLM • ATHENS • TOKYO • MILAN
MADRID • WARSAW • BUDAPEST • AUCKLAND

ISBN 0-373-11885-6

NO PLACE FOR LOVE

First North American Publication 1997.

Printed in U.S.A.

CHAPTER ONE

'ROSES?' Hugo, sprawled in the threadbare armchair in his sister's dressing-room, glanced up as Fred, the ageing major-domo who guarded the stage door as if it were the entrance to some sacred temple, appeared in the doorway with a huge cellophane-wrapped bouquet. 'Red ones, too. Who's your secret admirer, sis?'

Lacey laughed merrily, taking the bouquet and making Fred blush by reaching up to kiss him on the cheek. 'No, it's just Clive—to wish me luck,' she responded, glancing at the card. 'Bless him—how thoughtful.'

Hugo snorted in derision. 'Just Clive, indeed! I'll tell you what, if you're not careful you'll find yourself splashed all over the Sunday papers— "Government minister in affair with actress." A *married* government minister at that. And a blonde actress, practically young enough to be his granddaughter. They'd just love it.'

'Don't be silly,' Lacey chided, her soft violet-blue eyes dancing as she smiled down at her handsome twin. 'I'm not having an affair with him.'

'I know that, and you know that,' Hugo countered sagely. 'But you can bet your sweet life the papers could make it look as though you were.'

'Well, I'm not going to stop being friends with him just because some nasty reporters have got smutty minds,' she declared forcefully. 'He's a very nice, very sweet man—I feel sorry for him. His wife hates living in London, and he has to be here while Parliament's sitting. He gets lonely.'

'Lonely my foot! He's nothing but a dirty old man. You certainly do pick 'em!'

'If you're talking about Ted Gardiner, you know that wasn't my fault,' Lacey protested, moving aside some of the clutter of make-up on the dressing-table to make room to lay down the bouquet. 'He seemed so nice—how was I supposed to know he was lying when he said he wasn't married?'

'That's your trouble,' her brother insisted. 'You think everyone's nice. If I weren't around to watch out for you, I don't know where you'd be.'

'Yes, and your idea of taking care of me nearly lost me this part!' she retorted indignantly. 'You can't speak to a producer like that.'

'I can when he's pestering my sister.'

'He wasn't pestering me—he just took me out to dinner a few times. And he was a perfect gentleman.'

'Except that he was married,' Hugo pointed out with a touch of asperity. 'And don't pretend that you don't know what he was leading up to—even you're not that naïve.'

Lacey conceded a wry smile. 'No—well, I suppose you're right. But it isn't the same thing at all with Clive. For one thing, he's almost sixty! And besides, if you annoy him, he might stop backing the play, and it isn't easy to find "angels" to put up the money these days.'

Hugo yawned, stretching lazily. 'Well, don't say I didn't warn you.'

'Oh, there's no harm in him,' she averred, running her hairbrush through the bright golden curls that tumbled around her shoulders. 'Besides, if he isn't worried about the papers getting hold of it, why should I be?'

'Because, my sweet, trusting little sister, you would be forever typecast thereafter as a career-wrecking, marriage-wrecking bimbo.'

Lacey gurgled with laughter. 'Well, I'm typecast already,' she pointed out without rancour, striking a pose in her stage costume—a low-cut, skin-tight red jersey and a black leather mini-skirt short enough to reveal an interesting inch of black stocking-top whenever she moved. 'Blonde hair and big boobs equals dumb—period. I could have a fantastic career if I didn't mind taking my clothes off in public.'

Hugo flashed her a wicked grin. 'Lucky one of us doesn't mind, then, isn't it?' he teased. 'Someone has to pay the rent.'

'I pay my share,' she countered indignantly. 'You don't *have* to be a *Sauvage* if you don't want to. Anyway, I thought you'd give it up once you'd got your degree.'

He shrugged wide, well-muscled shoulders, tanned to a deep, healthy bronze and shown off to striking effect by the sleeveless black T-shirt he was wearing. 'Why should I?' he queried laconically. 'It's great, getting paid to have hundreds of girls screaming for my body.'

'Prancing around on stage wearing nothing but a couple of bits of leather and a few chains?' she chided, shaking her head. 'I do wish you'd get a proper job.'

'Oh, I will, one day,' he conceded with a yawn. 'I told you, once I've saved up enough money to start my own business, I'll—— '

'Two minutes to curtain, Miss Tyrell,' the assistant stage manager called from the corridor.

'Oh, lord! Do I look all right, Hughie?' Lacey begged, casting an anxious glance at her reflection in the huge, brightly lit mirror over the dressing-table and dabbing her nose with a little more powder.

'Well,' he mused, surveying her with sardonic amusement, 'it's a good job you're not planning to walk down the street in that outfit—you could cause a traffic accident.'

'I know,' she sighed wryly, wriggling to adjust the clinging jersey so that it didn't skim quite so low over the lush curves of her breasts. 'It was bought in for Vanessa, and she hasn't got quite as much up top as me.'

'Well, just be careful you don't bend over too far in it,' he advised. 'You're likely to pop out.'

Lacey giggled. 'That'd make sure we got a full house for the rest of the week, wouldn't it?' she remarked, checking her appearance one last time before skipping out to take her place in the wings and await her cue.

She was under no illusions that understudying the role of French au pair in a rather weak comedy being produced in a converted West London bus station was going to prove her big break. She only had the part for a few days anyway, while the actress who was supposed to be playing it recovered from a bout of flu.

It wasn't exactly a demanding role; it mostly required her to stand around looking alluring, and adjusting her suspenders, as the household of her employers disintegrated around her. The husband had most of the laughs—when they came. But it was better than resting, and serving behind the counter in the local fast-food emporium, as she had for the previous six months.

The house sounded even thinner than usual, and it was hard work to get as far as the interval. With a sigh of relief, Lacey hurried back down the passage to her dressing-room. Hugo was still draped across the armchair, reading the evening paper.

'I thought you had a date tonight?' she queried, slanting him a questioning look as she slipped behind the screen to change into her costume for the second act—a frivolous pink silk wrap, trimmed with a froth of swansdown.

Hugo yawned, casually tossing aside the paper. 'There's no rush,' he drawled with all the arrogance of handsome youth. 'It does 'em good to keep 'em waiting.'

She frowned at him in stern reproach, but with little hope of being attended to. Much as she loved her twin brother, she couldn't help disapproving of his behaviour sometimes. But then if his girlfriends were silly enough to put up with it . . . ! She knew she had been lucky to have had him around to put her wise to the dangers of falling for any smooth masculine lines as she was growing up—she could certainly never say she was unaware of the pitfalls!

'What time will you be coming home?' she asked, checking her stockings for runs as she took them across to the tiny washroom opposite her dressing-room to rinse them through ready for tomorrow—the company wasn't large enough to afford more than one wardrobe mistress, and she had more than enough to do.

'I don't know,' she heard him call back. 'Don't wait up for me.'

She chuckled with laughter, leaning over the sink to splash cold water over the pulse-points of her wrists and throat—she found it always cooled her down after the heat of the stage lights. 'If I waited up for you every time you stayed out half the night, I'd never get any sleep!' she chided him as she walked back into her dressing-room.

'Is that so?'

She stopped abruptly. A total stranger was standing in the middle of the room, regarding her with insolent disdain; a tall stranger, with crisp dark hair, wearing an immaculately cut grey suit which moulded his wide shoulders to perfection.

'Who the . . . ?' She glanced around in confusion. 'Where's Hugo?'

'If you mean the young Adonis with his hair in a ponytail, I just passed him in the corridor,' the stranger responded. 'Miss Tyrell?' He allowed his dark gaze to slide down over her body, taking in every contour on the way. 'Yes—you're exactly the type I expected.'

Her eyes flashed in anger, and she glared back at him, uncomfortably aware that the loose wrap was displaying rather too much of the soft shadow between her breasts. 'Really?' she queried, discreetly easing the swansdown lapels a little more closely together. 'And what type is that?'

'I believe you know exactly what type I mean, so please don't waste my time with that pretence of injured innocence,' he countered with caustic contempt.

She stared up at him, startled by such unwarranted hostility. She had never met this man before in her life—she was quite certain that she would have remembered if she had; that hard-boned, arrogant face, with its faintly patrician nose and firm, level mouth wouldn't be easy to forget.

'I . . . I'm sorry,' she managed, struggling to project a facade of cool dignity. 'I'll have to ask you to leave—the public aren't allowed backstage in the middle of a performance.'

'Oh, I'm not the public,' he responded, his voice menacingly soft. 'You could call me a sort of friend of the family. Does the name Jon Parrish mean anything to you?'

She frowned. 'Of course. He's Clive Fielding's . . .' Realisation dawned with a bump. '*You're* Jon Parrish?'

'Correct,' he confirmed tautly. 'Sir Clive Fielding's stepson.'

Lacey faltered, not quite knowing how to respond. Somehow they seemed to have got off on entirely the wrong foot, but it wasn't too late to put it right. She tried a smile, though it was a bit of a wobbly effort. 'Well, how do you do? I . . . I'm very pleased to meet you . . .'

'I haven't come here to exchange pleasantries, Miss Tyrell,' he rapped tersely. 'And I'll warn you now that you'll be wasting your time trying to play off your tricks on me. My taste has never run to well-stacked blondes—and even if it did I'm a bit too awake to the time of day to be taken in by a cheap little gold-digger like you.'

The stinging insult almost took her breath away. 'You ... What?' she protested in furious indignation. 'How dare you speak to me like that?'

Again that indifferent regard swept down over her, and she found herself wishing that she was wearing rather more than this flimsy wrap. With her curvaceous figure, she was accustomed to having men stare at her—drool over her, to be more accurate. But apparently the promise of her firm, ripe breasts, dainty waist and shapely *derrière* did nothing for him.

'I've heard a great deal about you, Miss Tyrell,' he informed her in a voice of cold derision. 'Apparently you specialise in rich men old enough to be your father. You had Ted Gardiner in your coils, beguiling him into giving you a part in his play—until you decided my stepfather was a better prospect. If I had my way, women like you would be horsewhipped.'

She glared at him, her palm itching to slap that arrogant face. 'Get out of here,' she demanded heatedly. 'Or I'll ...'

'You'll what?' he countered with biting mockery. 'Have me thrown out? I doubt it—I'm a good friend of the producer, not to mention the stepson of one of your most important backers. I'll go when I'm good and ready.' He leaned back casually against the edge of her dressing-table, asserting his intention to stay as long as he pleased. 'Nice roses,' he remarked, casting them a sardonic glance. 'From my stepfather? Or that macho hulk who was leaving as I arrived? No, he wasn't the type to buy flowers.'

'They're from your stepfather,' she retorted, returning him a defiant glare. It was more than apparent that losing her temper with him was going to get her nowhere—a more subtle approach was needed. Deliberately she picked up the flowers, sniffing delicately at their sweet fragrance. 'Mmm, lovely—they must have cost a fortune, out of season like this.'

Those dark eyes kindled in momentary anger. 'You little tramp,' he grated. 'I'm warning you, your affair with him is over.'

She blinked at him in shock, controlling with difficulty her boiling anger at his unwarranted assumption. 'I'm afraid you're under a misapprehension,' she informed him coldly. 'I'm not having an affair with Clive. He's simply a friend.'

He laughed in chilling scorn. 'You really can't expect me to believe that,' he sneered. 'It may be less than flattering to your ego, but you're just the latest in a very long line—mostly blonde, and mostly as...opulently endowed as you. His taste in mistresses is quite tiresomely predictable.'

She slid him a glittering glance from beneath her lashes. It was evident that he had come here without speaking to Clive first. Well, he deserved to be taught a sharp lesson about jumping to conclusions about people; three years in drama school had taught her plenty about improvising characterisations.

Strolling across the room, she disposed herself gracefully in the shabby armchair, crossing her slender legs and letting the wrap slip a little to display a few tempting inches of creamy thigh. Smiling with just a hint of coyness, she shook back her hair, lifting one hand to rub the nape of her neck, knowing how the movement would cause her firm, round breasts to rise beneath the soft silk of her wrap. She was pleased to note that he couldn't help looking, though his dark eyes conveyed only mocking contempt.

'You're not a very dutiful stepson,' she pouted, a husky laugh in her voice.

'I have no particular reason to be—my stepfather has never done anything much to earn my respect. But you had better believe, Miss Tyrell, that I have no intention of allowing him be dragged into a scandal over a cheap little tart like you.'

She had to force herself to ignore that barb. 'Why don't you call me Lacey?' she purred, her violet eyes peeping at him from beneath the silky fringe of her lashes. 'Everyone does.'

'I wouldn't care to be that familiar, Miss Tyrell,' he grated with deliberate emphasis. 'Oh, and by the way, if you have any ideas about selling your sordid little kiss-and-tell story to the gutter Press, you can think again.'

She lifted one delicately arched eyebrow. 'But I'm sure they'd be very interested,' she demurred provocatively. 'It's just the sort of juicy little titbit they love. If I play my cards right, I could make a great deal of money.'

She had the satisfaction of knowing that she had driven him to the very edge of losing his temper; it was costing him a visible effort to regain his control. 'It would be very dangerous for you to cross me, Miss Tyrell,' he warned, his voice soft and sinister. 'I have a great deal of power—rather more, in fact, than most politicians. You might discover that any money you make wouldn't go very far if you were never to find another job—not even cleaning floors.'

Lacey felt a small chill scud down her spine; she was quite sure that he could—and would—carry out such a threat. She knew, from the things that Clive had said, that even he was slightly in awe of his stepson. She couldn't quite remember what line of business he was in, but she knew he was highly successful at it. Now she had met him, she wasn't at all surprised—he was completely ruthless.

He was watching her in silence, those hard eyes glinting. But she'd be damned if she'd let him intimidate her! She was quite enjoying playing out her role—by the time she had finished with him, he was going to owe her the biggest apology of all time!

'Tell me,' she queried, deliberately goading him, 'what does your mother think about Clive's...er—mistresses?'

But he had himself well in hand again now. 'My mother gave up allowing herself to be concerned a very long time ago,' he responded with cool restraint. 'They came to an agreement to lead virtually separate lives. So long as he was discreet, she didn't mind what he did—naturally a divorce could have been harmful to his career.'

'How very civilised,' she approved bitingly.

'Perhaps. However, I will not have her subjected to public humiliation—she has been unwell recently, and I don't want her to have to cope with that sort of strain.' There was an unmistakable thread of steel in his voice. 'I believe I have made myself clear, Miss Tyrell—and rest assured, these are no idle threats.'

'Oh, no?' It was time to call an end to this little game! Rising to her feet, she regarded him with frosty dignity. 'Well, let me tell you something, Mr Super-Powerful Jon Parrish. If you had bothered to speak to Clive before you came round here throwing your weight around, *he* would have told you what I told you—we are not, repeat *not*, having an affair. We are simply friends—though I doubt if your smutty little mind can conceive of such a thing. Nor do I have any intention of speaking to the Press. Now will you kindly get out of my dressing-room? You're polluting the atmosphere.'

He had listened to her speech with an air of sardonic amusement, and as she finished, he slowly clapped his hands in mocking applause. 'Well done, Miss Tyrell,' he taunted. 'A magnificent performance—almost worthy of an Oscar.'

She stared at him in angry frustration. He hadn't believed a word she had said! And then he stood up and came towards her, those dark eyes glinting with unmistakable menace. She stepped back in alarm, but in the small room there was nowhere to go.

With an abrupt movement he caught both her wrists, shackling them in steely fingers, and jerked her against him. 'Maybe I can understand what my stepfather sees in you after all,' he grated softly. 'When your eyes flash like that, they add a certain spirit to your whole face.'

Before she had realised what he was going to do, he had tangled one hand in her hair, dragging her head sharply back, and as she gasped in shocked protest his mouth descended on hers in a kiss that was almost savage in its intensity.

She struggled to be free, but beneath that air of aloof urbanity he had portrayed was the hard-muscled strength of any primitive male, angry and aroused. And to her shame, she felt herself responding, succumbing helplessly to his fierce demand, melting in a honeyed tide of purely feminine submissiveness.

His lips were moving over hers, hot and enticing, as his tongue plundered deep into the sweet, defenceless valley of her mouth. Her head was dizzy from the racing of her blood, and she was clinging to him as his hand slid down the length of her spine to mould her supple body into his hard embrace.

His other hand had shifted to encompass the rounded fullness of her breast, cupping and caressing it with an insolent assumption of licence. But she couldn't control the sudden flare of heat he had ignited inside her. Her tender nipple had ripened to an exquisitely sensitive bud beneath the delicious abrasion of his palm, the teasing touch of his fingers, as electric sparks of pleasure crackled along her nerve-fibres and pierced her brain.

And for one magical moment it seemed as though he too had been caught up in the same wild surge of desire; his kiss gentled to the most incredible tenderness, and their bodies seemed to melt together like two halves cast from the same mould.

She heard herself moaning softly, her head tipping back into the crook of his arm as his hot mouth roved over her trembling eyelids and down to the delicate shell of her ear, his hard teeth nibbling sensuously at her lobe and making her shiver with heat...

The voice of the assistant stage manager calling the end of the interval shattered the spell. Jon drew back, regarding her with acute distaste. 'Well, that's one thing you can't cover up with acting,' he sneered, wiping the back of his hand over his mouth as if to wipe away every last trace of her. 'You really are nothing but a cheap little tart.'

With a sudden rush of shame, Lacey realised that the tie of her silk wrap had slipped loose, affording him much too generous a glimpse of the warm fullness of her breasts, somewhat inadequately contained in the delicate lacy cups of her bra. Her cheeks flamed scarlet, and she snatched at the wrap, tying it tightly around her waist, all too aware of the way it outlined every curve of her body.

'Get out of here,' she hissed.

'Don't worry—I'm going,' he countered witheringly. 'Forgive me if I can't bring myself to sit through the second half of the play.' He deliberately let his gaze drop to the rounded curve of her breasts, rising and falling in her heated agitation, the taut buds of her aroused nipples still faintly visible beneath the sheer fabric. 'I think I've seen more than enough of your talents.' And turning on his heel he strode out of the room, closing the door behind him with a controlled slam.

Lacey felt herself trembling inside. The humiliating memory of that kiss seemed to be burned on to her mouth like a physical scar—and she wasn't sure that it would ever go away.

But she had no time to pull herself together—she was due back on stage. Pausing only to repair the worst ravages to her make-up, she hurried down the stairs, crossing her fingers that he had meant it about not staying for the second half; she didn't like the idea of him sitting out there in the darkened auditorium, watching her, unseen . . .

Lacey sat at the kitchen table, idly toying with her breakfast. She had slept little, and now she seemed to have lost her appetite. Disturbing images of what had happened last night were still troubling her brain. How on earth could she have let him kiss her like that? It had been stupid of her to taunt him—like baiting a wild tiger.

The yellow gingham curtains at the window gave the illusion of bright sunlight streaming into the room, though in fact it was a dull November morning, drizzling with rain. The kitchen was spotless; it had been Hugo's turn to clean it up yesterday, and he always tackled the chore with a thoroughness that amused her—it was just a pity he couldn't be more tidy in between.

She glanced around, sighing a little wistfully as she let her chin rest in her cupped hand. Their mother would have been pleased to see that they were keeping the little flat the way she would have wanted it. She had always been very houseproud, though it hadn't been easy for her, a widow with two children, working long hours in the kitchen at the local hospital.

It was almost three years now since she had died; Lacey often thought that Hugo had taken it harder than she had, though he didn't say much. But every time she visited the neat little cemetery where their parents were buried side by side, there were fresh flowers on the grave, and she knew that he had been the one who had put them there.

'Morning, sis.' Hugo himself, clad in a pair of hip-hugging denim jeans, his magnificently muscled torso bronzed and bare, strolled into the kitchen, yawning and rubbing the back of his head with his hand. 'What's that you're eating?' he teased her cheerfully, looking askance at the contents of her cereal bowl. 'It looks like wet cardboard.'

'It's muesli,' she informed him with dignity. 'You should try it—it's good for you.'

He shook his head. 'Can't call that a proper breakfast,' he insisted. 'Let me see . . .' He opened the fridge, scanning the contents. 'It's full of your damned live yoghurt! Haven't we got any bacon?'

'Bottom shelf.'

'Oh, yes—thanks . . .' He took the packet out, tossing it on to the worktop beside the cooker, and reached into the cupboard to find the frying pan. 'Hope I didn't wake you when I came in last night,' he remarked. 'It was pretty late.'

'Oh . . . No, I was fast asleep,' she lied a little self-consciously. 'Did you have a nice time?'

He shrugged. 'So-so. I reckon I'm going to cool that one off a bit. She's starting to get . . . Hey, you damned mutt! He's got the bacon!'

He threw himself across the room, trying to rugby-tackle a spring-loaded bundle of yellow fur that darted nimbly out of his way and dashed off down the hall, triumphantly bearing his prize.

'Khan! Bad dog—give me that!' Lacey scolded, the effect of her stern words somewhat mitigated by the laughter in her voice. The overgrown pup peeped out from beneath his shaggy yellow fringe, weighing up his chances of escaping a second time as Hugo closed in on him.

The ensuing tussle had them all landing in a heap on the floor, Khan barking excitedly and trying to lick them both, his tail flailing wildly. Hugo pushed him off, struggling to sit up.

'Damned animal! Look at that—three rashers, and he's eaten the lot! Call him an Afghan? He's a greedy pig, that's what he is!'

'Ah, don't hurt his feelings!' Lacey protested, hugging the dog and letting him shower slobbery kisses over her cheek. 'He can't help it—he had a disturbed childhood.'

Hugo laughed, pushing himself to his feet. 'He saw you coming! You're nothing but a soft touch for any waif and stray that crosses your path.'

'Well, but I couldn't let them have him put down, just because they couldn't cope with him any more,' she argued. 'I know he's a handful, but he'll grow up one day, and then he'll be beautiful.'

'When?' enquired Hugo with a touch of asperity. 'I don't see much sign of it so far. He doesn't even look like an Afghan, with that silly fringe—in fact he's the stupidest-looking dog I've ever seen.'

'Don't take any notice of him,' Lacey advised the dog earnestly. 'He's only jealous 'cos you're better-looking than he is. Want a cup of tea?' she added to her brother. 'I was just going to——' A loud ring at the doorbell interrupted her. 'Oh, it's probably the postman—I'll get it.'

The scuffle with the dog had loosened her dressing-gown a little, and she held it together with one hand as she went to open the door. Unfortunately Khan had come along to see who it was, and at that exact moment Mrs Potter, who lived in the flat opposite, came out with her little West Highland terrier on its lead.

Khan gave a bark of fury at spying his mortal enemy, and Lacey had to grab his collar swiftly to restrain him from his murderous intentions. Her dressing-gown fell open, revealing her softly curvaceous figure, clad only in the skimpy baby-doll nightdress she wore in bed. But it wasn't the postman at the door—it was a photographer.

'Hey!' She gasped in shock as a flashbulb dazzled her eyes. 'What the hell do you...? Khan, get *in*!' Wrestling with the dog prevented her from covering herself, and the photographer managed to get several more very revealing shots before she could do anything about it. By the time she had got the dog under control, the man was inside the door, along with another carrying a small tape-recorder.

'Miss Tyrell? John Brennan, *Sunday Beacon*—this is my colleague, Roger Williams. We just want to ask you a few questions. Is it true that you're a friend of Sir Clive Fielding, the MP? When did you meet him? How well do you know him?'

She stared at them in bewilderment. 'Yes, I know him,' she responded, managing at last to bundle Khan into the nearest room and shut the door on him—causing him to howl as if he had been cast out into the uttermost darkness. 'But it's none of your business...'

'Did you know he was married, Miss Tyrell?'

Her violet-blue eyes flashed in icy indignation. 'Yes, of course I knew—he told me so the first time we met. But there's nothing wrong in it—we're just friends... Hey, where do you think you're going?'

The reporter had spied the bouquet of roses on the hall table—she hadn't yet got around to putting them in a vase. Dodging past her, he snatched up the card that had come with them. 'What's this? "Wish I could be with you tonight. Fondest love. Clive",' he read in a mocking tone. 'Just friends, eh?'

'Give me that!' she protested, lunging for the card, but he held it out of her reach.

'We're going to publish, Lacey,' he taunted, his manner sneeringly over-familiar. 'But you could be on to a nice little earner here if you're a sensible girl. We're willing to offer you fifty grand for the exclusive.'

Lacey almost exploded in fury. 'How dare you come in here asking your filthy questions?' she spat at him, a hectic flush colouring her cheeks as she realised her dressing-gown was still gaping open, revealing rather too many of her charms. She clutched it around her body, putting up her arm to shield her face as the photographer raised his camera again. 'Get out of here.'

'You want more money? Sure—sixty wouldn't be too much.'

'I'm not going to talk to you! Now get out of here, before I call the police.'

'Lacey...?' Hugo appeared in the kitchen doorway, looking incongruously domesticated with an egg in one hand and the spatula in the other. 'What the hell...?' He took one look at the reporters, and sized up the situation. 'Get out,' he growled. 'Unless you want your legs broken.'

Since he looked perfectly capable of carrying out his threat—they weren't to know what a complete pussycat he was—the two men retreated strategically towards the door. 'This your boyfriend, is it, Lacey?' the one with the tape-recorder enquired intrusively.

'I'm not answering any more of your questions,' she raged.

'OK, OK—just one last picture, eh, Roger?'

The flashbulb exploded again—catching Lacey still clutching at her loose dressing-gown, Hugo's arm protectively around her shoulders. Hugo bellowed in rage, and pounced after them, trying to grab the camera, but they were very nimble—no doubt through long practice—and were gone before he could catch them. He chased them down the steps, but they had a car waiting, and all that happened was that they got more pictures of him hurling the egg at the car and yelling wild threats as it swerved away.

He came back up to the flat to find Lacey in tears. He wrapped his arms around her comfortingly. 'Hey, don't let the bastards upset you, love,' he coaxed as she sobbed her heart out against his chest. 'It isn't worth it.'

'They made me feel so dirty, and I haven't even done anything wrong,' she protested brokenly. A sudden thought struck her. 'Oh, my lord, I ought to ring Clive and warn him...'

'I should imagine he knows all about it by now,' Hugo advised her acidly. 'And he'll be thinking only of how to save his own skin—he won't give a damn about you. Now come on, stop crying—you'll make your eyes all red and puffy.'

Lacey sniffed, reaching for the roll of kitchen paper and tearing off a piece to wipe her eyes. 'You were right,' she admitted wryly. 'I should have listened to you. But I never thought the papers would really be interested, even if they found out about us.' She frowned. 'I wonder how they *did* find out?'

Hugo shrugged. 'It wouldn't take much—politics is a very dirty game. A bit of rivalry inside the party, or someone out to take a dig at the government... They're just using you, I'm afraid—you happened to be convenient.'

Lacey stared up at him, shocked. 'Do you really think so? But that's awful!'

He laughed, hugging her affectionately. 'Dear old Lacey—how have you managed to live in this world for twenty-two years and remain so innocent? Most people would... Damn, what's the matter with that stupid hound now?'

'Oh, dear—I shut him in the bathroom. I was afraid he'd get out and chase Mrs Potter's dog, and she's already threatened to report him to the police as dangerous.'

She hurried to open the bathroom door. Four and a half stone of half-grown Afghan hound launched himself past her, scampering round in a circle in the middle of the hall and then diving into the living-room to leap on to the sofa, his brown eyes liquid and appealing, accusing her of the most ruthless cruelty for shutting him up for so long.

She couldn't help laughing. 'You rascal—you know you're not supposed to be on there,' she scolded him fondly.

From the bathroom came an angry roar. 'That damned dog! He's had my shaving-brush now! I swear one day I'll strangle him!'

CHAPTER TWO

AFTER that unpleasant experience, Lacey would have liked nothing better than to be able to shut herself in her room and hide. But if there was one thing guaranteed to take her mind off her troubles, it was the youngsters at the day centre where she worked part-time as a drama therapist. All of them had been classified as having severe learning difficulties, but their enthusiasm for the Christmas play they were preparing was enormous.

'It's really coming on,' remarked Hilary, the centre manager, watching as some of the cast earnestly rehearsed a scene. 'And they really seem to be enjoying themselves.'

Lacey nodded. 'They wrote most of the script themselves, by improvising,' she explained quietly. 'It's about Jesus coming back in the present day, as one of the homeless in London.'

Hilary looked impressed. 'Who thought of that?'

'They did,' Lacey responded proudly.

'Very good. Let me know what you're going to need in the way of props and scenery, and I'll see what I can do.'

'Thanks,' Lacey whispered. 'That was very good, Tom,' she added, raising her voice to the characters on the makeshift stage. 'Maria, I like the way you're sitting, but could you just turn a little this way, so we can see your face properly?'

27

'Was I really good, Lacey?' Tom queried excitedly, his eyes alight with pride.

'You were *very* good,' she asserted with emphasis. 'And you've learned your lines really well. Well done.'

'I know my lines too, Lacey,' Maria put in eagerly, coming over to take her hand.

Lacey smiled down at her with warm affection. 'Do you? You have been working hard. We'll come to your bit in a minute. I want you all to practise your song first, OK? Come on, gather round the piano.'

It made her feel warm inside to see all their bright, happy faces as they clustered around her. Sometimes it made her really angry that life seemed so unfair to them, but when she thought about the way that people who apparently had so much more could be so arrogant and rude, she was inclined to the conclusion that they were the ones to be envied.

The day centre was only a short distance from the flat she shared with Hugo, and with a speculative glance at the grey November sky she decided to walk home instead of waiting for the bus. It took her rather longer than she had expected—she had lived in this part of south London all her life, and it was inevitable that she would keep bumping into people she knew. By the time she had stopped to chat, nodding in sympathy at the story of someone's recent spell in hospital, congratulating someone else on the birth of a new grandchild, it was beginning to rain.

She had to pop into the small supermarket on the corner to get a bottle of milk and some dog food for Khan, and then hurried the rest of the way home, struggling with her umbrella and her shopping, cursing mildly at a car that splashed her as she waited to cross the road.

As she turned the corner, she noticed with surprise that the same car was drawn into the kerb outside her block of flats. She frowned, puzzled. It was a sleek dark blue Aston Martin—who on earth could be visiting around here, driving a car like that? At least she could be fairly sure it wasn't another reporter.

The driver was still at the wheel, and as she drew closer an uncomfortable suspicion began to dawn in her brain. A glimpse of a dark head and a pair of wide shoulders in an immaculately cut jacket confirmed it; it couldn't be anyone else but Jon Parrish.

Well, he needn't think she was going to stop and speak to him, after the way he had behaved last night! Ignoring him completely, she climbed the flight of steps to her front door on the first floor, irritated at her own uncharacteristic clumsiness as she struggled with her umbrella and her shopping and fumbled for her keys.

She heard him open the car door. 'Miss Tyrell?'

Her umbrella was slipping, and instinctively she tried to catch it, succeeding only in dropping the bottle of milk. It smashed on the step, spilling broken glass and milk in the rain. 'Oh . . . drat!' she muttered, juggling with the tins of dog food as they too began to slip out of her hands.

He came quickly up the steps and took them from her before she dropped them.

'Oh . . . Thank you,' she responded, automatically polite, but instantly jumped back on to the defensive before he could think she was making any concessions. 'What are you doing here, anyway?' she demanded, glowering up at him in undisguised suspicion.

Those dark eyes glinted, warning that he hadn't come to apologise. 'We need to talk,' he answered tersely.

'We have nothing to talk about,' she insisted, trying to reach the lock with her key while still holding on to all the things she was carrying.

'Unfortunately we do,' he ground out, taking the key from her. 'As you may be aware, the newspapers have discovered your relationship with my stepfather.'

'I told you last night, I don't have a relationship with your... Look out!'

He didn't heed her warning, and as he pushed the door open he found himself mobbed by an over-excited bundle of fur, not sure whether to attack him or try to lick his face.

'Khan—down!' Lacey instructed sharply, afraid that if her dog ran to meet her he would cut his paws on the broken glass. She hurriedly shooed him back inside, catching her open umbrella on the door and muttering more impatient curses.

Jon calmly took it from her, shaking off the rain-drops and closing it down as he followed her into the passage. 'Sit,' he instructed Khan imperiously.

To Lacey's absolute astonishment, the delinquent hound immediately responded by plopping his back end down on the floor, his front paws neatly together, his whole expression conveying smug pride in his own uncharacteristic obedience.

'Good lord—how on earth did you get him to do that?' she queried, forgetting all her wariness in her surprise.

Just for a moment, a smile flickered at the corners of his hard mouth, and Lacey felt her heart give an odd little flutter; that smile was quite startlingly attractive. But she couldn't afford to let herself think like that, she reminded herself sharply.

'Well, you'd better come in,' she remarked, the inflection of sarcasm in her voice acknowledging that he had already done so.

'Thank you.' He closed the front door behind him. Khan, evidently deciding he was a friend, was fawning at his feet, his rump in the air, his curly tail wagging wildly. 'What exactly *is* this?' he enquired, restraining the exuberant hound as he reared up to seal their relationship with his floppy pink tongue.

'He's an Afghan hound,' she informed him, dumping the dog food on the kitchen table.

'Is that a fact?' He followed her into the kitchen. 'I'd have taken him for a mobile hearthrug.'

Lacey had to suppress ruthlessly the inclination to feel that anyone who could win Khan's adoration so swiftly couldn't be all bad—she could hardly rely on that brainless mutt as a judge of character, she reminded herself with a flash of wry humour.

She slanted him a wary glance from beneath her lashes. The memory of last night was still all too vivid in her mind, and although nothing in his manner now suggested that he was planning a repetition, she wasn't at all sure she should have let him across the threshold. She was going to have to handle the situation very carefully, avoid doing anything that he might take as further confirmation of the conclusion he had leapt to so readily last night; at least having her own clothes on should give her a little more confidence.

'Take a seat,' she invited stiffly.

'No, thank you,' he responded in clipped tones. 'I won't be staying more than a few moments.'

Biting back a sharp retort, she shrugged her slender shoulders in a gesture of pure indifference. 'Suit yourself,' she returned breezily. 'But first I'm going to have to go and clear up that mess outside, before someone hurts themselves.'

Without waiting for him to answer, she took the dustpan and brush from the cupboard under the sink and, stepping briskly past him, went out to the step to sweep up the broken glass. The rain had already washed the milk away, and it was running down into the gutter in a long white stream. She was going to have to go out and get another bottle now, or there wouldn't be enough for breakfast—thanks to that damned man.

But at least those few minutes had given her some valuable time to compose herself. When she went back inside, he was sitting at the kitchen table, and although she tried to ignore him she was conscious of those dark eyes following her as she carefully tipped the shards of glass into an empty cornflake packet so that the sharp edges wouldn't be dangerous, before stowing them neatly in the dustbin, and putting the dustpan and brush away.

'Would you like a cup of tea?' she offered, shrugging off her outdoor coat and tossing it across a chair.

He shook his head. 'No, thank you.'

'I could make you coffee instead?' If he was going to be churlish, she would retaliate with an excess of good manners.

His eyes flickered with something that could almost have been amusement, and he conceded a terse nod. 'Black, no sugar.'

She smiled sweetly, reflecting that he was fortunate she had no arsenic to put in it. She took her time about making the drinks, forcing herself to maintain that façade of cool indifference to his presence. It wasn't easy; she was quite used to having the kitchen filled with handsome hunks of male—Hugo's friends from the polytechnic, or the others in his all-male dance troupe. But there was something distinctly different about this man; he seemed to dominate his surroundings without any conscious effort.

The kettle boiled, and she made the drinks, bringing them over to the kitchen table, and sitting down opposite him. 'So—what was it you wanted to talk about?' she enquired, regarding him levelly across the table.

'Have you spoken to any reporters from the *Sunday Beacon*?' he demanded without preamble.

'They've been here,' she responded cautiously.

'I see.' His expression was grim. 'And did you give them an interview?'

'No, I didn't.'

He eyed her with frank scepticism. 'Did they offer you money?'

'Yes, as a matter of fact they did,' she informed him loftily. 'And I turned it down.'

That hard mouth curved into a faint sneer. 'Not quite enough for you, was it?' he taunted.

Her violet-blue eyes flashed with anger. 'Just what do you think gives you the right to come round here insulting me?' she exploded hotly. 'Just because I'm not rich and *powerful* like you, that doesn't mean you can treat me like a piece of dirt.'

'You placed yourself in that position when you chose to begin an affair with my stepfather,' he countered scathingly. 'You can hardly expect me to treat you like a lady.'

She felt a sudden urgent desire to throw her hot tea in his face, and had to force herself to put down her cup, her hand shaking slightly. 'Have you asked Clive about this so-called affair?' she asked, her voice very controlled.

'Naturally—and, like you, he denied it. Unfortunately, my stepfather's denials tend to have a rather hollow ring after all these years. And if I had had any remaining trace of doubt,' he added, letting his eyes drift down to the firm, round swell of her breasts and linger there with deliberate insolence, 'it would have been very thoroughly eliminated last night.'

Lacey could feel her heart beating faster, and was uncomfortably aware that beneath her pale blue sweater her tender nipples were ripening to hard nubs, as if in some kind of instinctive response to his dominating male presence. 'It wouldn't have made any difference what I'd done,' she countered defensively. 'You'd already made up your mind about me before you even came to the theatre.'

'True,' he conceded, a cynical twist to his mouth. 'I'd already heard a great deal about you from Ted Gardiner's wife—she happens to be my cousin. You really don't care what sort of harm you do, so long as you get what you want, do you? I have to admit, you're a very tempting baggage. But if you had any ideas of adding me to your list of conquests, I'm afraid you're in for a disappointment—the thought of touching you after Clive's had his paws on you is rather more than I can stomach.'

'Oh? You didn't give that impression last night,' she threw at him in ragged desperation.

He laughed without humour. 'Put that down to...curiosity,' he conceded. 'I can assure you I had no intention of allowing it to go any further.'

'Neither did I!' she snapped.

'No?' he enquired, coolly mocking. 'Well, we won't debate that one. But I don't imagine that a woman who could go to bed with a man old enough to be her grandfather can afford to possess a great deal of discrimination.'

'How many times do I have to tell you?' she demanded, her temper boiling over. 'I was *not* having an affair with him! I've met him maybe half a dozen times. He came backstage at the theatre, he took me out for coffee once or twice, and bought me flowers— that's all. What do I have to do to convince you?'

He leaned back in his chair, his dark eyes regarding her levelly across the table, and she found it impossible to read their expression. What was he thinking? Under that cool scrutiny she felt her cheeks flushing a hot pink, and had to look away from him. Why should she care whether he believed her anyway? He meant nothing to her; so far as she was concerned, she would be heartily glad if she never saw him again.

'Actually, it really doesn't matter whether I believe you or not,' he pointed out with cool indifference. 'My only concern is what the newspapers will be able to make of it. Once the *Beacon* breaks the story, the rest'll be swarming all over this place, offering you the sort of money that'll make the *Beacon*'s opening bid look like chicken-feed.'

'Then I shall tell them exactly what I told the *Beacon*,' she countered tautly. 'That I have no intention of speaking to any of them.'

His hard mouth twisted into a cynical smile. 'Oh, they can be pretty persuasive with their cheque-books—especially when they think they've caught a whiff of scandal in high places. I could really hardly blame you for being tempted. That's why I don't want you here where they can work on you—you're going to have to disappear for a few weeks, until the heat dies down.'

She shook her head, her thoughts flying instantly to Tom and Maria, and the other young people at the day centre. 'I can't do that—I'm involved in a play.'

He waved her objection aside with a dismissive gesture. 'I'm afraid you'll have to pull out of it—I doubt if they'll have much trouble finding a replacement.'

She glared at him, infuriated by his high-handed arrogance. And of course he had believed she was talking about her magnificent role in that paltry comedy. Well, she wasn't going to enlighten him—she was too angry with him, and she didn't want to give him the chance to mock at something that was so important to her.

'I don't care,' she asserted forcefully. 'I'm not going. I've done nothing to be ashamed of, and I'm not running away.'

Those dark eyes glinted in sharp annoyance; clearly he wasn't accustomed to having his commands disobeyed. 'I thought I had made myself clear, Miss Tyrell. I don't want you talking to the press——'

'And I thought I had made *myself* clear, Mr, Parrish,' she retorted, refusing to be intimidated by his high-handed manner. 'I'm not budging from this flat, and there's nothing you can do about it—unless you're planning to have me ... What's the term they use in the security services? Taken out?'

He conceded a flicker of sardonic amusement. 'I'm not connected with the security services, Miss Tyrell—nor was I proposing to use violence. If you insist on staying, I cannot prevent you. Although you could find yourself regretting your decision come Sunday,' he cautioned drily. 'You're likely to find the gentlemen of the Press less than gentle in their attentions.'

She tilted up her chin in haughty defiance. 'I'll cross that bridge when I come to it,' she declared, with a confidence she didn't quite feel.

'I don't think I need to remind you of my warning,' he remarked, his voice quite cordial but unmistakably laced with steel. 'If I find that you've been playing games with me, I shall make sure you regret it for the rest of your life.'

'I wouldn't dream of trying to play games with you, Mr Parrish,' she responded in saccharine tones. 'To be perfectly honest, I don't feel that this sort of cheap publicity would be of any use to my career.'

He seemed to weigh up her words, his dark eyes regarding her in narrowed calculation, but apparently she had at least partially convinced him. 'Very well,' he conceded, finishing his coffee and rising easily to his feet. 'If you should change your mind about my suggestion——'

'I won't.'

He took a small white business card from his pocket, and dropped it casually on to the table. 'If you should change your mind,' he reiterated with restrained impatience, 'call me.'

She glanced at the card with studied lack of interest. 'Even if I do decide to go away, I won't come to you for help.'

That hard mouth curved into a taut smile. 'Believe me, Miss Tyrell, your distaste for our brief acquaintance can hardly be stronger than my own; nothing would please me more than the assurance that we would never have to meet again. Unfortunately, however, I fear that things aren't going to prove quite that simple.'

'So far as I'm concerned they are,' she returned with a snap. 'I wish I'd never met you—or your stepfather.'

'It's a little late for regrets now.'

'I never expected all this trouble to come out of it,' she maintained crossly. 'I just felt sorry for him—he seemed so lonely.'

'No doubt he told you that his wife didn't understand him?'

'He told me she wasn't interested in politics, and didn't like living in London,' she returned with dignity.

'So you offered to comfort him?'

'No! I just . . . I thought we could be friends, that's all.'

He laughed without humour. 'Spare me the protestations, Miss Tyrell. No one could be so naïve as to think a man of Clive's age would be interested in mere friendship with such a nubile young thing as yourself. You knew full well what he was after.'

Lacy felt her cheeks flush a heated pink—she *had* been that naïve. If Clive had been younger... But if the thought had even crossed her mind, she would have dismissed it as ludicrous.

'At least you have the grace to blush,' he taunted, taking her embarrassment as proof of her guilt. 'And I trust you'll heed my warning—it would be very unfortunate if you should force me to take action against you. Good afternoon.' He bid her farewell with a terse nod.

Khan, suddenly realising that he was leaving, scampered out into the hall after him, wistful brown eyes shamelessly imploring him to stay and play. He indulged him briefly with a tickle in just the right spot behind his floppy ear, leaving him besotted, gazing in abject despair at the front door as it closed.

'Khan, don't be stupid—come here,' Lacey called, her voice shaking slightly.

The dog padded back to her, as miserable as if the bottom had fallen out of his whole world, and pressed his drooping head against her knee. 'You daft mutt,' she comforted him softly. 'You really took to him, didn't you? But he's not a very nice person, I'm afraid. I thought dogs were supposed to have some kind of instinct about these things?'

The intelligent hound lifted his head, eyeing her rather doubtfully, and then slurped her cheek with his pink tongue.

'Ugh! Get off!' she protested, laughing as she pushed him away. 'How many times do I have to tell you not to lick my face?'

But though she wouldn't care to admit it, even to her four-legged confidant, she felt a strange sense of dejection herself. What was wrong with her? She had never met such an insufferably rude and arrogant man in her entire life. The very last thing she wanted was to be forced to have to see him again.

Vanessa was back in the role of French au pair by Saturday—however ill she might be feeling, she would never dream of allowing a mere understudy to take her place for the main performance of the week. So Lacy was relegated once again to helping out with the props and making coffee for the stage manager and the director. Which was probably just as well, she acknowledged wryly to herself—it would be difficult to cope with even such an unexacting role when she was fretting herself ragged with worry about what the Sunday papers were going to contain.

If only she *could* disappear! But where could she go? Apart from an elderly aunt who lived in Tooting, she and Hugo had no other relatives that they knew of. And she couldn't impose on the hospitality of her friends—she had no idea how long this was going to last, and if the Press found out where she'd gone it could cause all sorts of problems.

Maybe it wouldn't be as bad as she feared, she tried to reassure herself over and over. After all, they didn't exactly have much of a story, based on the facts, and there were laws of libel to prevent them publishing outright lies—weren't there?

The rest of the cast were going off to a party after the show, but she couldn't bring herself to join them, pleading a headache. Ted, the producer, was there, waiting to convey them off in his Rolls-Royce, and he drew her to one side.

'You do look a little pale,' he agreed, a note of agitation in his voice. 'Are you worrying about this thing with Clive getting into the papers?'

She nodded. 'It's probably stupid—there's nothing they can make anything of.'

'You didn't tell them anything about me, did you?' he asked anxiously.

She shook her head angrily, exasperated by his self-centredness. 'No, I didn't. I didn't tell them anything.'

He beamed in relief. 'Are you sure you don't want me to take you home and tuck you up in bed?'

'No, thank you,' she asserted quickly—she could all too readily guess that his idea of tucking her up was likely to include tucking himself up with her!

'Well, see you next week then,' he conceded, drifting off reluctantly with the others.

She smiled wanly to herself. She was quite sure that if things turned out as badly as she had feared he wouldn't hesitate to dump her from the production. Well, it wouldn't be much of a loss, she assured herself wryly—there had to be something better than playing understudy to French au pair!

The flat was in darkness when she got home—Hugo was performing with *Les Sauvages* at some nightclub in Croydon. She undressed, and went straight to bed, but she couldn't sleep—there were too many unwelcome thoughts buzzing in her brain. After tossing and turning restlessly for several hours, she finally threw back the bedclothes and, reaching for her dressing-gown, padded out into the kitchen to make herself a mug of hot cocoa.

It was there that Hugo found her when he came in half an hour later—sitting at the kitchen table, her head in her hands. 'Hi, sis,' he greeted her with a wry grin. He tossed a copy of the *Sunday Beacon* on to the table in front of her. 'I picked it up on the way home,' he explained. 'You ain't gonna like it.'

The banner headline screamed out at her: 'Minister in Blackmail Plot.' Beneath it was a picture of Clive in Downing Street, looking as kindly and respectable as a bishop, and one of herself taken the other morning, carefully cropped to make it look as if she had been a willing subject, posing provocatively in her underwear, displaying a more than generous amount of cleavage, pouting for the camera. A cold chill wrapped around her heart as she picked it up and read the story.

'I don't believe it!' she gasped, stunned. 'How can he have said this? It's the most awful pack of lies I've ever heard! He's told them that I approached *him*, that I kept pestering him, that he was only friendly with me because he felt sorry for me—and that I started demanding money from him, and threatened to claim we'd been having an affair if he didn't pay up!'

'It looks as if he's decided to try and make a last-ditch attempt to save his own skin by throwing you to the wolves,' Hugo remarked caustically. 'I did warn you.'

'Yes, but...*this*! How can a person be so... *dishonest*? And he seemed such a nice old man.'

Hugo laughed drily. 'You're such an innocent!' he teased with gentle affection. 'I don't know how you manage it in this dirty old world, but you never seem to be able to think badly of anyone.'

Lacey's soft mouth twisted into a wry smile. There was *one* person she thought badly of—but she had been doing her best to forget about Jon Parrish for the past few days. Not that it was easy; the unwelcome memory of their two brief encounters tended to flit back into her mind far too frequently for comfort.

Khan, sensing something was wrong, had heaved himself up from his beanbag in the corner and came over, laying his long nose in her lap and gazing up at her from beneath his yellow fringe with liquid brown eyes that held nothing but simple adoration. She stroked his tousled head absently.

'Why can't people be more like dogs?' she questioned wistfully. 'They're so...uncomplicated. I'm sure the world would be a better place.'

Hugo snorted. 'Not if they were all like that stupid mutt—he hasn't an ounce of brain in his whole body. Do you know he got hold of a packet of cotton-wool while you were out yesterday afternoon, and ripped it up all over the sitting-room floor? It took me ages to pick it all up.'

'Oh, is that where it went? You naughty dog!' Khan accepted the compliment with delight, jumping up to lick her face and trying to climb on to her lap. 'No—hey, you can't do that! You're much too big,' she protested, laughing in spite of her distress. 'Ow! Your claws are digging in me! Get down!'

'Is that cocoa you're drinking?' Hugo enquired with a wide yawn. 'I think I'll have some too.'

She slanted him a teasing look, struggling to be brave. 'Going to bed with a mug of hot cocoa? Whatever would all those girls who've been screaming all evening for your hunky body say if they knew?'

He chuckled with laughter. 'It would ruin my image! I'll have to make sure it doesn't get out.'

Lacey cast a wry glance at the newspaper on the table. 'A couple of days ago, I would have laughed at that,' she mused with dejection. 'But now...' She picked up the paper again. 'They've called you my "mystery lover" in this, and they've got a picture of you chasing those reporters down the steps. It's a bit fuzzy, though—I don't think anyone would recognise you. I don't suppose it would do any good to tell them you're my brother?'

He shook his head grimly. 'I doubt it.'

'Could I sue them for libel, do you suppose?'

He sat down opposite her, taking the paper from her and scanning the page. 'I don't know. It would be pretty difficult, with that old git having told them all this rubbish—it would be your word against his.'

'And they'd be much more likely to believe him.'

'Exactly. And it would cost a fortune.' He put the paper down. 'It doesn't look as if there's much you can do.'

'That's what I was afraid of.'

It was a couple of hours before Lacey could get to sleep, and it seemed as though she had barely closed her eyes when there was a knock on the door. 'Who the . . . ?' She groaned, rolling over to peer sleepily at the clock. It was a quarter to six. Who on earth . . . ?

There was another loud rap on the door, and the letterbox rattled. She sat up sharply. Khan had woken, and raced out into the hall, barking ferociously and scrabbling at the door. And that would have Mrs Potter complaining, she realised with weary resignation, dragging herself out of bed and putting on her dressing-gown.

She knew who was at the door. Reporters. No doubt all the other papers had picked up on the story, and now they would all be trying to get their oar in. Well, she had no intention of opening the door to them—she had learned that much at least during her short period of notoriety.

'Lacey?' Someone was calling through the letter box as she stumbled out into the hall. 'Come on, love—we know you're in there. Just let us in.'

'No—go away,' she protested, her voice choked with angry tears. 'I'm not going to speak to you.'

'Ah, come on—be a sensible girl. We're not from the *Beacon*—that's just a comic anyway, no one's going to believe what they print. We'll give you a chance to tell *your* side of the story. And we'll pay you. Come on, what do you say?'

'I said no,' she reiterated raggedly. 'Go away.'

'How much did they offer you? Fifty thousand? Sixty? We'll give you eighty. That's eighty thousand quid, right in your hand. And you can tell us whatever you like.'

She didn't even deign to answer, grasping hold of Khan by his collar and dragging him back to the kitchen.

'A hundred thousand, Lacey,' followed her as she walked away from the door.

Hugo had woken too, and came storming out into the hall, his temper close to snapping. 'You get away from that door,' he bellowed, 'or I'll come out there and *really* give you something to write about, you lying bastards!'

There was a muffled scuffle outside, and it seemed the reporters had decided that discretion was the better part of valour. But they didn't retreat far. The next call was from downstairs, outside the window. 'Lacey...? What are you afraid of? If you've got nothing to hide, you've got nothing to lose by coming out and talking to us.'

'Oi! What's going on down there?' Lacey sighed, and sank her head into her hands. Mrs Potter was awake, and not best pleased about it. 'Go on, be off with you—waking decent people from their beds in the middle of the night. If my George—God rest him—was still alive, he'd give you a piece of his mind. Now get away with you, before I come down there with my broom!'

'My lord! They don't know what danger they're in!' chuckled Hugo, strolling into the kitchen and putting on the kettle. 'I'm afraid you're going to have to get used to this, love—lord knows how long they'll be camping out there. We might as well have a cup of tea.'

CHAPTER THREE

By TEN o'clock in the morning, there were more than a dozen pressmen hanging around at the foot of the steps. A small crowd of neighbours had gathered, agape with blatant curiosity, and a couple of policemen had arrived to keep the peace. The telephone had been ringing all morning—there had even been calls from a couple of public relations people, offering to act as her agent; in the end they had had to unplug the telephone from the wall.

Besieged in the flat, Lacey was pacing up and down in restless agitation. 'Oh, God, I can't go on like this,' she ground out. 'How long are they going to stay out there? I'm not even going to be able to go to work tomorrow—I can't have them trailing me down to the day centre and hanging about like this there!'

Hugo, sprawled on the settee watching an ancient re-run of *The Lone Ranger*, glanced up. 'You'd better give Hilary a ring and let her know you can't go in,' he suggested.

She nodded. 'Yes, I will. And I'm going to ring Clive as well,' she added grimly. 'This is all his fault. If he's got a shred of decency in him...'

Hugo snorted with derisive laughter. 'That's the triumph of hope over experience!' he commented in a voice laden with cynicism. 'He's a politician—they don't know the meaning of the word!'

She was beginning to think he was right. But nevertheless she was still prepared to give Clive one last chance; after all, there could have been some misunderstanding—the reporters had quoted her own words very selectively to cast the worst possible light on their so-called interview with her.

Her hand was shaking slightly as she dialled his number. The phone was picked up almost immediately, and her heart gave a sharp thud as she recognised the brusque voice that barked, 'Yes?'

'J...Jon?' she stammered. 'I... This is Lacey—Lacey Tyrell...'

'It's hardly likely to be any other Lacey, under the circumstances,' came the sardonic retort. 'What do you want?'

'I want to speak to Clive,' she responded, her anger sparking at his mockery.

'Well, I'm afraid you can't. He isn't here.'

She hesitated, a little taken aback. 'Where is he?' she asked.

'I've despatched him for a short holiday.' The voice was cool, with an unmissable undertone of ruthlessness. 'He's gone abroad.'

'Oh...' She sat down heavily. It was quite evident that Jon Parrish had taken control of the situation, and intended to run it his way. It was a measure of his power that he was able to dictate to his own stepfather—what chance did she stand of fighting him?

'I'm surprised you've left it so long to call,' he remarked, an inflection of lazy mockery in his voice. 'I was expecting to hear from you first thing this morning.'

'There didn't seem to be a lot of point,' she responded bitterly. 'After Clive had told the newspapers that pack of lies ... I'm only ringing him now because I'm desperate—there's a whole crowd of reporters outside the door, and I can't even go near the window.'

'I dare say you'll have some of the contingent that have been here joining you shortly,' he responded with a hint of acerbic amusement. 'Once I'd managed to convince them that their quarry had flown, they'd be looking for other prey.'

'Very funny!' she snapped, her patience sorely tried. 'It's all right for you—you probably live in a great big house with a wall all round it, and if you need to you can hire people to do everything for you. I'm stuck here with them howling right on my doorstep, and the neighbours are complaining already.'

'I did advise you to get out of town,' he reminded her drily.

'I never dreamt it was going to be like this! I've never been in the papers before. And I thought—foolish of me, I suppose—that Clive would at least have the decency to tell the truth. Instead he's made me out to be the worst kind of blood-sucking bitch imaginable.'

He laughed without humour. 'If you couldn't take the heat, you should have stayed out of the kitchen.'

'Oh, I know I'm wasting my time talking to you!' she spat. 'You'd never lift a finger to help me in a million years.'

'On the contrary,' he responded evenly. 'Our interests coincide—you want to get away from the

Press, and I want to get you away from them. Fortunate, don't you think?'

'It might be for you,' she retorted, her voice taut with annoyance. 'Anyway, where am I supposed to go? They'll find me wherever I try to hide.'

'Oh, I think I know somewhere suitably remote for you to stay.' His tone suggested that somewhere in Outer Mongolia would scarcely be far enough away for his liking.

'You needn't think I'm going anywhere you'd choose to send me,' she countered hotly.

'Suit yourself...'

He sounded as if he were about to put the phone down, and she swiftly had second thoughts; after all, she couldn't sit here like a prisoner indefinitely, and she had no one else to turn to. 'No—wait,' she pleaded urgently. 'I... All right. But how am I going to get out without them following me?'

'We'll have to smuggle you out from under their noses.' He was silent for a moment—she could almost hear that sharp, calculating brain ticking over. 'You're an actress,' he mused. 'Could you put on some sort of disguise?'

Lacey blinked in surprise. 'Y...yes—at least, I think so...'

'Good. Where would be the best place for me to meet you?'

She hesitated for a moment, thinking. 'There's a pub on the main road—the Rose and Crown, just a little way down from my turning. It's got a car park— I could meet you there.'

'Fine. Shall we say in one hour?'

'An hour. Yes . . . All right.' She really didn't have much choice, much as it galled her to let Jon Parrish have his way. She couldn't stay here, that much was certain—all the neighbours would be complaining to the council, and they could end up getting evicted!

'Good.' His voice was as coolly restrained as ever. 'If there are any difficulties, you'll be able to reach me on my mobile phone—the number's on the card I gave you. Do you still have it?'

'Y. . . yes,' she admitted; she had been going to throw it away, but somehow it had found its way on to her bedside table, and had stayed there even though she had twice tidied up.

'Until later then,' he concluded, blandly businesslike. 'Goodbye, Miss Tyrell.'

She put down the phone, and sat glowering at it as if it were responsible for everything that had gone wrong. She was wishing she had never heard of Jon Parrish—let alone his stepfather!

And now she had been forced to do exactly what he wanted. A small shiver ran through her. She might have known he would get his own way in the end—his sort always did. Perhaps it was just as well that he believed she had been having an affair with Clive, at least if it meant that he wouldn't be interested in her himself.

'How do I look?' Lacey demanded, emerging from the bedroom.

Hugo rolled his eyes expressively heavenwards. 'Awful! Like Mrs Potter on a bad day.'

She gurgled with laughter. 'Well, I just hope it does the trick. Now, don't forget to make sure there aren't any dogs in the street before you let Khan off his lead.'

'Don't worry. We'll do the business, won't we, lad?'

Khan, delighted at playing such an important role in this conspiracy, wagged his tail wildly.

'And make sure they're not following you,' she added anxiously. 'It'd be a bit of a waste of effort if they find me after all this.'

'Did you actually tell the fellow you were bringing the dog along too?' Hugo enquired, slanting her a quizzical look.

'Well, no—not exactly,' she admitted. 'But I couldn't leave him behind—he'd pine.'

'*He'd* pine? If he has one more pair of my trainers, I swear I'll choke him to death.'

The accused hound gazed up at him, the picture of injured innocence. Lacey chuckled. 'No, you wouldn't—you love him really. But anyway, I don't know how long I'm going to have to stay away, and you've got that gig in Manchester on Friday. It's best if I take him with me.'

'Right. Well, I'll meet you beside the pub in ten minutes. Ready? Good luck.'

She nodded, crouching low as Hugo made ready to open the door. Khan, scenting freedom, was off like a rocket, barking joyfully and causing as much distraction as anyone could desire. Lacey slipped out of the door as Hugo closed it behind him, and darted swiftly up the steps to the top floor, where in a minute she would show herself very prominently, hoping that all the newsmen would assume she had come from one of the upstairs flats.

It worked like a dream. Padded up to look as if she weighed fifteen stone, with her giveaway golden hair tucked beneath a grey wig and a plastic rain hat, wearing a dowdy old raincoat and clumpy shoes, she was unrecognisable in the gloomy winter drizzle. She had packed some clothes into an old tartan shopping-trolley, which she used to good effect to draw attention to herself as she laboured down from the second floor, muttering impatiently.

No one took the slightest notice of her as she trundled past—it apparently didn't occur to any of them to look twice at this plump, elderly housewife, or wonder where she was going on a Sunday, with her shopping trolley obviously full; they were looking out for a curvaceous blonde, and were blind to everything else under their noses.

She made it to the rendezvous exactly on time, to find Jon's car already there. He too seemed not to see her as she approached, and the look of astonishment that registered in his eyes as she tapped on his windscreen made her smile in smug satisfaction.

'*Lacey*?' he queried. 'My goodness, I . . . I would never have recognised you!'

'That was the general idea,' she pointed out. 'Can the trolley go in your boot? It's got my clothes and things in it.'

He glanced at it askance, but climbed out of the car and helped her load the unwieldy thing into his beautifully carpeted boot. She felt a twinge of guilt at the muddy marks made by her wheels; what on earth was he going to say when he saw Khan?

He closed the boot, and walked round to open the passenger door for her, inviting her to climb in. She hesitated, glancing around anxiously—Hugo should be here by now...

'What are you waiting for?' he enquired with a hint of impatience. 'You don't want to hang around here for too long or someone might see you.'

'I know, but... Oh, it's all right—here they are.'

Khan had clearly been having a wonderful time on his short walk; he was prancing along, pleased as punch with the mud that caked his oversized feet. As he trotted along at Hugo's side he was looking all around him, alert for more mischief, but as soon as he spotted Lacey he darted forward, greeting her as ecstatically as if he hadn't seen her for weeks.

She hurried over and took his lead. 'Was everything OK?' she enquired a little breathlessly. 'They didn't suspect anything?'

'Not a thing!' Hugo asserted. 'I had a bit of trouble getting him back on the lead, though—he got into someone's front garden and started digging up their roses before I could catch him. But it was OK—I got him away before they spotted him.'

'Thanks.' She stood up on tiptoe and planted an affectionate kiss on his cheek. 'Look after yourself—I'll see you when I see you.'

'Same to you. Better not try and ring me...'

'Pardon me for interrupting this touching farewell,' came a sardonic voice from behind them. 'But am I to understand that you're proposing to bring that... animal with you?'

'Er... yes.' She flickered him an uncertain smile. 'I'm sorry, I know he's a bit muddy—Hugo let him run loose, you see, to distract the reporters outside the flat, and he got into someone's garden...'

'He's not getting into my car.'

Hugo had melted strategically away, leaving the two of them to confront each other. Khan, recognising a friend he had met before, had darted forward to the full stretch of his lead, and Lacey struggled to haul him back, anxious that he shouldn't compound the problem by getting his muddy paws all over Jon's expensively-tailored grey suit.

'I have to take him,' she insisted. 'I can't leave him behind—I couldn't expect Hugo to look after him ...'

'But he's absolutely filthy!'

'I know. I'm sorry. I'll ... I'll clean your car for you afterwards ...' she offered diffidently.

Some people had arrived at the bus stop on the opposite side of the road, and were watching with mild curiosity the odd couple arguing beside the elegant car. With an exclamation of annoyance, Jon opened the rear door, and Khan skipped inside, sniffing the luxurious pale grey Connolly leather upholstery before deciding that he had finally arrived at his proper station in life, and settling down on the seat, his paws neatly crossed and his head held regally erect, inviting admiration.

Jon snorted in disgust, and walked round to climb in behind the steering-wheel, leaving Lacey to slip into the passenger seat and close the door herself. From beneath her lashes, she slanted a wary glance up at his set profile; at least she had got her own way—but at what cost?

Lacey waited until they were well away from her district before dragging off her wig with a sigh of relief and removing the padding from her cheeks.

'Phew...that was uncomfortable,' she remarked, hauling out the pillow that had given her such an upholstered figure from beneath her voluminous raincoat, and stowing it away behind the seat.

Jon glanced down at her, a faintly sardonic smile hovering at the corners of his hard mouth. 'A very effective disguise,' he remarked drily. 'I take it our friends from the Press were well deceived?'

'Completely!' She gurgled with laughter, her violet-blue eyes dancing with wicked amusement. 'You should have seen it when Khan went bounding down the steps at them!' she gurgled. 'He only wants to play, of course, but you'd have thought he was the Hound of the Baskervilles the way they all jumped out of his way.'

The dog, who had been comfortably dozing on the back seat, lifted his head at the sound of his name, and panted with pleasure.

'I trust he isn't going to add drooling to the general mess he's making of my upholstery,' Jon remarked caustically.

'He doesn't drool,' Lacey protested, indignant on behalf of her pet.

He flickered her a doubtful glance. 'How exactly did you come by such a monstrous creature?' he enquired.

'The people who owned him couldn't manage him. They were actors, and I think they'd got him just for the glamorous image—they didn't realise how much work they take to look after. Anyway, someone told me they were going to have him put down, and I *couldn't* let that happen. So I adopted him. I've had him nearly a year—he's almost two now.'

'And what does your boyfriend think of him?'

'My boyfriend?' For a moment she stared at him blankly. 'Oh, you mean Hugo!' An instinct of self-preservation suggested to her that it might be useful to let him go on thinking Hugo was her boyfriend. 'Oh, he doesn't mind him,' she responded airily.

'How remarkably forbearing of him!'

They drove in silence for a while, Lacey gazing out of the window as they swung around the roundabout on to the broad dual carriageway of the A20, heading for Kent. She had never ridden in a car like this before. With an idle finger she traced the pattern in the gleaming burr-walnut on the dashboard fascia. One day, if she ever became a successful actress, she would have a car like this...

Again she caught the sardonic glint of Jon Parrish's dark eyes, and sat back quickly in her seat. 'Where are we going?' she enquired, an odd trace of unsteadiness in her voice.

'Northumberland.'

'Northumberland?' Lacey flashed him a look of indignant protest. 'Couldn't you find somewhere a bit further away?'

He smiled in acerbic humour. 'I'm afraid it's not very glamorous—no showbusiness parties or slavering sugar-daddies to wind around your little finger. In fact it's miles from anywhere. One of my companies owns some property in Redesdale—an old farmhouse. It's being converted into holiday flats, but at the moment it's empty. It seemed the most suitable retreat for you.'

'Thank you,' she responded, her eyes glittering. 'It sounds simply wonderful. How long will it take to get there?'

He shrugged his wide shoulders in a non-committal gesture. 'We should be there by late afternoon—it depends on the traffic.'

'As long as that?' She stared at him in horror. 'But I'm starving—I hardly ate any breakfast this morning.'

He nodded, the faintest flicker of amusement passing behind his eyes. 'We'll stop for lunch on the way,' he conceded. 'I know a place a little way off the motorway where it should be a bit quieter. The fewer people who see you, the better.'

She sank lower in her seat, her pretty nose wrinkling in disgust.

He slanted her a quizzical look. 'What's wrong?'

'I feel like a fugitive,' she grumbled mutinously.

'I could point out that you brought it on yourself. That was a very fetching photograph in the papers, by the way. You didn't tell me you'd posed for them.'

Her eyes flashed him a spark of fire. 'I didn't—they took that as I was opening the door. I didn't even know they were there.'

He laughed without sympathy. 'You don't seem to have found the Press as easy to deal with as you anticipated,' he remarked. 'I hope it's taught you a lesson.'

'I made the mistake of trusting your stepfather,' she retorted bitterly. 'I thought he was a sweet old man—and he's turned out to be a complete rat.'

'Yes, well, I won't disagree with you on that point,' he conceded. 'Next time you set out to find yourself a sugar-daddy to have an affair with, you'll have to be a little more careful.'

'For the last time—I was *not* having an affair with him,' she threw at him with considerable heat. 'Not that I care what *you* think, anyway.' She tilted up her chin, turning her head away from him. '*I* know the truth, and that's all that matters to me.'

'You sound like Mary Poppins,' he taunted, those dark eyes flickering over her in a lazy mockery. 'The appearance, however, somewhat belies the image.'

'I can't help the way I look,' she retorted with frosty dignity.

His laughter was soft and cynical. 'No, I don't suppose you can.'

As it was a Sunday afternoon, the orbital motorway around London was fairly quiet, and they made good time, leaving the M1 a little way past Leicester to drive into a small town a few miles further on. They parked the car and, leaving Khan snoozing peacefully on the back seat, went to have lunch in the restaurant of a nearby hotel.

It was exactly the sort of place she would have expected him to patronise: quietly elegant—the sort of place that would never serve prawn cocktail or steak more than medium rare. No one took any notice of them as the head waiter led them over to one of the best tables in the room.

'I can recommend the duckling,' Jon advised, glancing down the menu. 'They do it with a very good pepper sauce——'

'I . . . don't eat meat,' she cut in diffidently. 'I'm vegetarian.'

'I see. Well, in that case why don't you try the mushroom and spinach roulade?' he suggested without missing a beat. 'I think you'll find that rather nice. Do you drink wine?'

'Just a little.'

'Then I suggest you have a glass of the house wine—
it's really quite pleasant. I'll have a glass of Perrier,'
he added to the waiter, 'with a slice of lemon.'

Lacey found herself fingering her napkin ner-
vously, and tucked her hands quickly into her lap.
She wasn't usually nervous with men—having grown
up so close to Hugo, she treated them mostly with the
same easy camaraderie she shared with him. Just oc-
casionally, one would take that as an invitation to be
over-familiar, but they quickly found out that her
looks belied her old-fashioned nature.

Perhaps it was hardly surprising that Jon shouldn't
have realised that, she reflected with an uncomfortable twist of shame—not after the way she
had let him kiss her. It would be quite a reasonable
assumption, from his point of view, that she was easy
with her favours; and from there it was only a small
step to believing that she would be willing to have an
affair with a married man more than thirty years her
senior.

He really wasn't a bit like Clive, she mused, studying
him covertly from beneath her lashes. The older man
projected an air of affability and easy charm, a desire
to be liked by everyone. But in his stepson there
seemed a total indifference to other people's opinions.
She couldn't imagine him ever stooping to court
popularity—everything about him seemed designed
to keep the world at arm's length; even his polished
good manners were part of the façade—like a sheet
of glass that stopped anyone getting close enough to
touch him. But there had to be a human being in there
somewhere—it just might take a little more effort to

warm him up. She tried a smile. 'Clive told me you run your own business,' she remarked brightly. 'He talked about you a lot, you know—he's awfully proud of you.'

'Really?' His eyes glinted with hard scepticism. 'I'm surprised you found time to discuss things like that.'

His implication was clear, and she felt a hot flush of anger rise to her cheeks. But she wasn't going to give up yet. 'He said it was something to do with farming?' she queried.

'That's right.'

'You don't look like a farmer,' she persisted, risking a hint of teasing.

'Don't I?' He lifted one dark eyebrow in quizzical enquiry. 'What does a farmer look like?'

'Oh, you know what I mean,' she argued. 'You look more like a banker or something in the City.'

'I'm based in the City,' he responded evenly. 'I own the land—I don't actually do the farming myself. That's the way most farming is done these days—it's the only way to make it viable.'

'Oh... That's a pity,' she mused, her violet eyes taking on a shade of wistfulness.

He laughed with dry humour. 'A typical Londoner—you see the countryside as some kind of theme park, with milkmaids and pretty lambs skipping about, don't you?'

'Well, I certainly don't like the idea of factory farming and battery hens,' she retorted hotly.

'I don't deal in livestock—all my holdings are arable land.'

'Oh . . .' Somehow she felt as if she had been fended off—the conversation had reached a stalemate. She tried a different tack. 'Are you married?'

'No. And I have no intention of answering a series of questions about my private life,' he added, his tone perfectly civil but underlined with a thread of steel.

Lacey lapsed into an awkward silence—she had been well and truly put in her place! Fortunately at that moment the waiter arrived with their lunch, so she was able to concentrate her attention on eating the delicious roulade instead.

But it was difficult to be unaware of the man sitting opposite her; he had a presence that many of the professional actors she knew—more conventionally handsome, many of them—would have envied. It was something to do with that intrinsic air of command, a familiarity with wielding power, coupled with an air of cool composure and reserve that made him seem above the common herd.

But she couldn't afford to let herself forget that that veneer of cultured urbanity had proved awfully thin the other day; when it had come to the crunch, he had exhibited the sexual instincts of a caveman.

Of course, that had partly been her own fault for provoking him so deliberately, she acknowledged with painful honesty. But it was still a long way to Northumberland, and there was no telling what might happen on the way. She was going to have to be extremely careful not to let it happen again.

'Are you ready to go?'

'Oh . . . Yes, of course.' Lacey flickered a slightly uncertain smile at the man across the table; there was something that had been bothering her ever since they had come into the restaurant, and she had realised that the prices were probably above her touch. 'That was a really nice meal. Er... Are we going to split the bill fifty-fifty?'

'Of course not.' Jon glanced across the room to catch the waiter's eye, and handed him a credit card. 'There won't be any food at the farmhouse, so we'll have to take some with us—I noticed there was a shop across the street that was open. You'd better go back to the car and wait—the fewer people who see you, the less chance there is of anyone recognising you.'

'Hadn't I better come with you?' she enquired. 'You might not know what to get.'

'I think I'm capable of chosing a selection of groceries,' he countered drily. 'Is there anything you particularly like or dislike?'

'No,' she conceded, chastened. 'So long as it's vegetarian. And don't forget dog food, will you?'

'I'm hardly likely to,' he responded with a glimmer of sardonic humour. He handed her his car keys. 'Try to keep out of sight as much as possible.'

She nodded, a wry expression on her face. How long was this game of hide-and-seek with the Press going to last? A week? A month?

Khan was delighted to see her, bouncing up and trying to poke his head through the narrow opening they had left at the top of the window. 'Stupid,' she chided him, laughing. 'You couldn't even get your nose through there. Come on, you'd better have a walk before we carry on—only try not to get your feet muddy again!'

She opened the door carefully, but the dog, frustrated at having been confined for so long, shot out of the car before she could catch his lead, and dashed off across the car park, barking merrily, announcing to the whole town that he had arrived and was ready for any mischief that was on offer.

'Khan!' Horrified that she was drawing too much attention to herself, she hurried after him. 'Here, boy—come!'

He spared her a fleeting glance over his shoulder that plainly said, 'Not likely,' and pranced off, pausing from time to time to investigate an interesting smell, but skittering out of her reach each time she almost caught him, teasing her to join in his game.

'Khan...' She knew that any trace of impatience in her voice would only make things worse, so she tried to keep her tone light and playful. She almost had him cornered when suddenly he darted past her, barking ferociously. Startled, she turned to see him hurling himself at a young lad who was just getting into a car, with every apparent intention of ripping him to pieces. 'Khan!'

'Help!' the lad screamed, terrified. 'Get him off me!' He scrambled out of the car, trying to run away, but the dog refused to let go; his hard white teeth were sunk into the lad's arm, and he dragged him to the ground, growling with a viciousness he usually reserved only for Mrs Potter's yappy little terrier.

People were rushing into the car park from everywhere as Lacey ran to try to grab her beloved pet before he could do the boy any serious damage. 'I'm so sorry,' she gasped breathlessly. 'Has he hurt you? He's never done anything like this before...'

'My *car*!' A man in a leather jacket was standing by the open door of the BMW the lad had been getting into, his expression one of shock. 'He was trying to steal my car! Hold him—don't let him get away! Someone get the police.'

Suddenly Lacey found herself at the centre of a crowd as several men caught hold of the lad. He struggled for a moment, but found himself outnumbered, and Khan was still showing himself more than willing to rejoin the fray, barking excitedly, tugging on the end of his lead as Lacey strained to hold him.

'Keep that dog off me,' the lad protested sulkily. 'He bit my arm.'

'You're darn lucky that's all you got,' the owner of the car warned him harshly. 'If I'd caught you first . . .'

'He's a very clever dog,' someone else remarked, indulging Khan's already inflated ego with such fulsome admiration. 'He must have known the lad was up to no good.'

'They have an instinct,' chimed in another, patting the jauntily-tilted head. 'There's a good boy. You deserve a reward for that. I'm going to fetch you a nice bone from the kitchen here. Would you like that?'

Khan agreed very readily that he would, slavering over it as soon as it appeared as if he hadn't been fed for a week. The sound of a siren warned of the approach of a police car, its blue light flashing as it turned into the car park. Lacey felt her heart sink; there was no way she was going to be able to retreat discreetly from the scene—and Jon was standing on the fringe of the crowd, a grim expression on his face.

She slanted him a look of apology, shrugging her slim shoulders helplessly; there was nothing she could do.

Two police officers got out of the Panda and came over, and everyone began talking at once, telling them what had happened. 'And this is the lady with the dog!' she was introduced with a flourish.

'Ah, yes, miss.' The policeman had his notebook out. 'And could I have your name, please?'

'Er...' She stared around helplessly, feeling herself trapped. 'I...'

It was inevitable. Someone had produced a copy of the *Sunday Beacon*, and was studying her photograph on the front page. Several others peered over his shoulder, nodding their heads. 'It is—it's her. You're the one in the papers, aren't you?'

There seemed no point in trying to deny it. 'Er...yes,' she admitted, her cheeks scarlet.

The confession met with a mixed reception from the crowd; most seemed inclined to be sympathetic, though several gave her sideways looks, quite ready to believe that she was no better than she ought to be. She glanced up to find Jon at her side.

'Well done,' he murmured, a sardonic edge to his voice. 'This is your idea of keeping out of sight, is it?'

'I'm sorry,' she responded wryly. 'I couldn't help it.'

He rolled his eyes heavenwards. 'I should never have let you bring that damned dog along...!'

'But he stopped that man's car being stolen,' she pointed out, instantly springing to the defence of her pet. 'You've got to admit, that was very brave of him.'

He cast a jaundiced eye at the hero of the hour, still contentedly gnawing on his bone. 'I admit nothing of the sort,' he countered with asperity. 'And if he thinks he's bringing that disgusting thing into my car...!'

CHAPTER FOUR

'I DON'T see how it's going to make any difference that people recognised me,' Lacey protested defensively; they were back on the road again, heading north, and still arguing about what had happened. 'It's not as if there were any reporters there or anything.'

Jon slanted her a sardonic look. 'You don't think one of those people might perhaps see the chance to make a few quid by ringing the *Beacon* and letting them know who you were with?' he responded with a touch of asperity.

'How would they know who I was with? I didn't give them your name.'

'True,' he acknowledged. 'Unfortunately, there aren't too many of these cars on the road—it won't take much for them to put two and two together and make five. Speculating about what you and I are doing apparently running off together should give them several days' entertainment.'

'Well, it was your idea,' she countered caustically. 'I never wanted to come with you. If I could have thought of another way to get the Press off my back, I would have done it.'

'And now you've guaranteed that they're on our track again,' he pointed out with a hint of dry cynicism. 'They'll have their spies out all over the country.'

'Well, you said this place was remote,' she reminded him tartly, settling down in her seat and folding her arms, turning her head away to watch the passing scenery. 'So they won't find me, will they?'

'Won't find *us*,' he corrected her, his mouth a grim line.

She shot him a startled look. 'U...us?'

'You didn't think I'd risk leaving you to your own devices, did you?' he queried in a voice of lazy mockery. 'I intend to keep tabs on you.'

'Oh...' She lapsed into silence, staring out of the window. It had never occurred to her that he planned to stay in Northumberland with her—she had assumed that with an important business to run he would want to get back to London as quickly as possible.

A small shiver ran through her. What else was he planning? From beneath her lashes, she studied that hard profile. True, he had behaved so far today as if nothing could be further from his desire than to let himself be tempted by the woman he suspected of having an affair with his own stepfather—but she hadn't forgotten that kiss. And cooped up together in an isolated farmhouse, miles from anywhere, who knew what could happen...?

Outside a drizzling mist was descending, but inside the car it was warm and extremely comfortable; the powerful engine made hardly a sound, and the efficient suspension soaked up every bump and hollow of the road. Lacey could feel herself drifting on the fringes of sleep, watching Jon's hands on the steering-wheel—strong, well-made hands...hands that had caressed her with a devastating expertise...

It would be a couple of hours yet before they reached their destination. Northumberland ... It had a romantic sound, but never having been north of Watford she had only the dimmest idea of what it would be like. Imagination painted a rugged landscape, of wild, windswept hills and ancient castles beneath a stormy sky...

And the farmhouse they were going to? A pretty little grey stone cottage, tucked into a fold of the hills—with green-painted shutters on the windows, and a cosy inglenook fireplace where they could light a huge roaring fire to drive away the chill of the November night, and picnic on the hearthrug as the wind howled around the chimneys...

As she slowly sank into the world of dreams, the scene flickered into life. Jon had opened a bottle of wine, and as they sipped it he smiled at her in the soft glow of the firelight.

'This is to make amends,' he murmured, his voice low and smokey. 'I know now that I was wrong about you—you aren't the sort of girl who would have an affair with a man like my stepfather. Do you forgive me?'

'Of course.' Her cheeks had flushed a delicate shade of pink, and she lowered her lashes shyly as he leaned towards her.

'I hope this will be the first of many nights like this, here in our own secret hideaway...'

She woke with a start as the car braked abruptly. Khan fell from the back seat, and yelped indignantly, scrabbling to get up again. Lacey peered out of the window, but she couldn't see a thing—it was dark and misty, and drizzling with rain, and they seemed to be in the middle of nowhere.

'What on earth . . . ?'

Jon had slammed the car into reverse, and as he swung fiercely at the wheel a shot rang out. Lacey screamed. A figure appeared in the headlamps, a crazy old woman in rag-bag clothes with wild grey hair and wilder eyes—and she was levelling a shotgun straight at the windscreen.

The car spun again, and the shot missed. The woman howled in fury, scrabbling in her pocket for more cartridges. 'Damn you, bloody bailiffs—you aren't going to evict me! I'm stopping right here, and nobody is going to move me, so see if they don't.' She was reloading the shotgun with a shaking hand. 'I'll see you all off—aye, and swing for it if I have to. This here's my home, and they'll take me off it in my box, and not before.'

'What's happening?' Lacey gasped breathlessly as the car shot backwards down a bumpy lane. 'Who was that?'

'I haven't a clue,' Jon responded grimly, concentrating on the most remarkable piece of stunt-driving she had ever seen. After several hundred yards he pulled off into a layby and killed the headlights, and reached for his mobile telephone.

He punched out a number, and waited impatiently for an answer. 'Richard? It's me.' Clearly there was no need to identify who 'me' was. 'I'm up at the Grainger Farm property—what the hell's going on here? I thought it was vacant possession, but there's some batty old hag taking pot-shots at us.'

The voice that came back was crackled with static but still just audible. 'Oh, dear. That'll be the old housekeeper—a Mrs . . . Dinsdale, I think her name is. Apparently she refused to move off the site when old Grainger sold it—she's been squatting in a caravan ever since.'

'Why wasn't I informed of this?' Jon demanded, a steely edge to his voice that warned of trouble for whoever had been incompetent. He paused briefly for an explanation. 'Just a minor detail! You didn't think it was worth bothering me about it! The legal department were dealing with it—you thought it had all been sorted weeks ago? Well, it seems that it hasn't— it's fortunate that she's not a very good shot, or we'd have been peppered.' He sighed with wry resignation. 'All right, Richard—I'm sorry to have disturbed you on a Sunday evening. I'll call you in the morning. Goodnight.'

He turned the phone off, and put it down. 'It looks as though I'm going to have to go and deal with this "minor detail" of Richard's,' he remarked, his hard mouth quirked into a faintly sardonic smile. 'Stay here.'

'Why don't we just go somewhere else?' Lacey suggested anxiously. 'There must be a hotel or something . . . ?'

'Not within twenty miles. And this fog has been coming down for the past half-hour—it'll soon be too thick to see your hand in front of your face.'

Lacey bit her lip, her eyes wide with anxiety as she watched him climb out of the car and walk slowly forward until he disappeared into the murky darkness. The fog had closed the world down to a claustrophobic zone of eerie silence; they could have been on another planet.

Khan began to whine, scrambling over into the front seat and trying to get out of the door. 'No,' Lacey scolded him, worried about the further damage his hard claws could wreak on the leather trim. 'Get back in the back.' But the dog obstinately refused, and with a sigh she took hold of his lead and opened the car door. 'Hush now,' she warned in a whisper. 'Don't bark.'

He immediately did just that, and proceeded to drag her off after Jon. She hauled on his lead, but he was absolutely intent, and she wasn't strong enough to hold him.

At the gate of the farm-yard, a terrifying sight loomed up out of the deepening fog. Jon was standing there, his hands raised to the level of his shoulders, trying to reason with the old woman, who was un-waveringly holding the shotgun on him. She hesi-tated, trying to hold Khan back, but he pressed forward towards the scarecrow figure, eagerly wagging his tail, dragging her with him.

But to her amazement, as the dog fawned forward, greeting her as if she were a long-lost friend, the old woman turned the gun aside, and stooped to put out her hand to him. 'Well, hello there, young fellow. You're a cute one, aren't you? Where did you come from, then?'

Khan promptly lolled his head into her hand, in-viting her to scratch the spot just behind his ear. With an audible sigh of relief, Jon relaxed, lowering his hands—but instantly she levelled the gun at him again.

'I warned you,' she snarled menacingly. 'You keep back.' Still keeping a cautious eye on him, she turned back to the dog. 'Well, what are you doing out here?' she enquired of him, chuckling. 'You don't look like no bailiff's dog to me.'

'He isn't,' Lacey put in a little breathlessly. 'We aren't the bailiffs. We're ... on holiday. We were just driving around and admiring the countryside when the fog started coming down. We wondered if maybe we could stay here for the night?' she added, injecting her voice with every ounce of warmth and friendliness she could muster.

'Oh, aye?' The old woman slanted her a searching look. 'Funny time of year to be spending a holiday,' she pointed out quite reasonably.

Jon stepped forward, a wary eye on the shotgun, and slid his arm around Lacey's shoulders. 'As a matter of fact, we're on our honeymoon,' he lied without shame. 'Aren't we, darling?'

Lacey almost choked as he gave her an intimate little squeeze, gazing down at her with every semblance of adoration. 'Y...yes. We...just got married yesterday,' she managed unsteadily.

'It was a whirlwind romance,' Jon added with what Lacey considered rather unnecessary elaboration. 'We could only take a few days' break, so we decided to come up here.'

The housekeeper eyed them both with shrewd scepticism, but to Lacey's relief she seemed to believe them. 'Well ... All right, you can come in then,' she conceded guardedly. 'I don't know what you're expecting, mind—the place has been let go to rack and ruin since old Mr Edward moved out, and I dare say it's pretty damp. Still, I don't suppose you'll mind that,' she added with a lewd chuckle. 'You'll be keeping each other warm.'

Lacey forced a tight smile, summoning all her acting skills to gaze up dewily into Jon's eyes. A flicker of amusement was lurking in them, and she felt her stomach muscles tighten as for one crazy, breathless moment she found herself slipping into the illusion that they *would* be snuggling up together, generating enough body-heat to keep out the bitterest November cold...

'We'd better go inside,' he suggested. 'You'll catch cold, standing around out here. And don't forget,' he added in a whisper close to her ear as he pretended to nuzzle her with connubial affection, 'you don't know her name.'

'Why on earth did you tell her we were on our honeymoon?' she hissed.

'I didn't think she was going to swallow the idea of us just taking a holiday in the middle of November,' he responded blandly. 'I'm afraid my brain's not at it's best when I've got a loaded shotgun pointing at me.'

Lacey slanted him a doubtful glance, not sure if she believed that—she suspected that he would be the kind to keep his cool under any circumstances. But it wasn't a very good time to argue about it, not with the old housekeeper still watching them with a shadow of distrust.

The fog had come down even more thickly now, and she was able to see only a little of her surroundings. So much for her romantic dream of an idyllic country cottage, she reflected wryly; the

building was a rambling ruin, surrounding three sides
of a muddy, unevenly cobbled yard. One wing must
have once been stables, but was now virtually derelict, and the main part looked little better—the
windows were dark and blank, and several of the roof-
tiles were missing, which didn't promise too well for
the state of the interior. Mrs Dinsdale's rickety old
caravan, shored up on bricks against the side of the
building, looked almost cosy by comparison.

A trickle of rain ran down her neck, and she
shivered, realising how cold she was after the warmth
of the car. At least once they were inside they could
light a fire—if they could find anything to light it with.
It seemed doubtful that there would be any coal or
firewood—and even more doubtful that the electricity would be working.

The old housekeeper had set the shotgun aside and,
fumbling beneath her apron, produced a large, old-
fashioned key. 'This was a spare one they never knew
I had,' she revealed in a conspiratorial whisper. 'I kept
it so I could still go in and keep the place properly.'

Lacey nodded solemnly, feeling an instinctive sympathy for the displaced old lady; she had felt the same
about their council flat when her mother had died—
even though it hadn't been much, it had been her
home, and it had been a huge relief when she had
found out that they would be allowed to stay on.

The ancient front door had warped in its frame,
and Mrs Dinsdale had to give it a well-practised thump
to get it open. A damp, musty smell welcomed them
into a square hall, with several doors leading off it.

'Wait a minute—I'll light a candle.'

There was the scratch of a match, and then a faint, flickering glow which showed walls covered in peeling wallpaper patterned with huge cabbage roses, and a grubby old rag rug covering the cracked lino on the floor. Ominous brown streaks ran down the walls, and some of the plaster had fallen from the ceiling.

Mrs Dinsdale clucked disapprovingly, giving the ancient walnut sideboard a quick wipe with the corner of her apron. 'I'm sorry about the state of the place— I haven't felt like getting around so much as I used to,' she explained apologetically. 'If I'd known you were coming, I'd have put the duster round a bit. Cleaned the windows, too.'

'Oh, no, we wouldn't want to put you to any trouble,' Jon assured her smoothly. 'It's very kind of you to let us in.'

'Yes, well, it's been empty for a bit,' the old house-keeper conceded, melting a little. 'Since old Mr Edward left. Sold out to some fancy firm in London. Not that I blame him—he needed the money. But they're not going to move me on,' she added, her voice grimly determined. 'Not even those stinking bailiffs. I told 'em, they come back here and I'll turn my shotgun on 'em again—and I will, too.'

He nodded with every appearance of genuine sympathy. 'But even so, I expect it must be lonely for you out here by yourself?'

'I'm used to it,' Mrs Dinsdale declared stoutly. 'I were born not three miles from here, and I've lived here all my life. Never been further than Whittingham, for the fair.'

'I believe there's some wonderful countryside around here?' Jon went on, disarming the wary old

lady with an exercise of easy charm that left Lacey
bemused—*she* had never seen any sign of it before.

Mrs Dinsdale nodded. 'Aye, if you're a keen walker
you've come to the right place. There's all sorts of
paths, and Roman remains. And you'd want to see
the reservoir—right pretty, it is, though not so much
at this time of year.'

Jon smiled. 'We'll have to ask you for directions.
But now I'd better go and fetch the car. I won't be a
minute.'

Lacey flashed him a look of alarm, nervous of being
left alone with the crazy old woman and the shotgun.
'Don't be long,' she pleaded, her tone that of the besotted bride.

Those dark eyes glinted with wicked amusement. 'I
won't,' he promised.

Khan was still cementing his friendship with the
housekeeper, rubbing his head affectionately against
her legs. Lacey tried a smile. 'He's...taken to you,'
she remarked cautiously.

The old woman chuckled. 'I'm fond of dogs. Old
Mr Edward always kept a couple of 'em—spaniels,
mostly. I've never seen one like this, though. Odd-
looking tyke.'

'He's an Afghan hound,' Lacey supplied. 'He's still
a bit of a puppy, and not very well-trained, I'm afraid.
I expect I'll have to be careful around here—are there
sheep nearby?'

'Not right close,' the old woman assured her. 'Not
till over by Scatton Law—that's a mile or two over
yonder.' She pointed vaguely to the east. 'But you
wouldn't want to be going over by there anyway,' she
added in sepulchral tones. 'It's haunted.'

'Oh . . .' In that isolated house, enshrouded in fog, with just the light of the flickering candle to see by, the housekeeper's conviction was hard to dismiss. Lacey was struggling to keep the conversation going anyway—it was difficult to think of anything to say without letting slip that she knew more than she was supposed to about the house and its circumstances. It was a relief when she heard the car draw up by the front door. 'Ah, here's my . . . husband,' she managed.

Jon came in carrying the bag from her shopping-trolley, and a small overnight bag of his own, which he put down on the floor. 'There. It's a really filthy night—we're lucky to have a roof over our heads.' He turned to the housekeeper, offering her his hand. 'Thank you once again for your kindness, Mrs . . . ?'

'Dinsdale,' she supplied, awkward at shaking hands with him—she clearly regarded it as above her station. 'But it was Edna to Mr Edward, and that's what I prefer, if you don't mind.'

'Edna,' he agreed solemnly. 'Well, I'm Jon, and my wife is Lacey.'

The old lady nodded, satisfied. 'Aye, well . . . I'd best be getting along. If you need anything, just you come and knock on my door. There's more candles in the kitchen dresser. Goodnight to you both.'

As she bustled out, closing the front door behind her, Jon laughed wryly. 'Well,' he commented with a touch of dry humour, 'it seems that stupid mutt of yours has his uses after all—he certainly helped to break the ice. I thought we were going to have a serious problem.'

Lacey returned him a frosty glare. 'It's hardly surprising she was so hostile,' she pointed out tersely.

'Anyone would be, with the bailiffs trying to turn them out of the home they've lived in for years.'

He lifted one dark eyebrow in mocking surprise at her attack. 'I didn't even know she was here,' he countered. 'I didn't deal with the transaction personally——'

'No, I don't suppose you did,' she rapped, her voice laced with contempt. 'You get other people to do your dirty work for you. How could you stand there being so nice to her, when you knew full well that you're the one who's causing all her problems?'

He slanted her a look of faintly sardonic amusement. 'What does it matter to you?' he challenged mockingly. 'You've no reason to care what happens to her.'

'I feel sorry for her,' she retorted. 'I know what it's like to be afraid of losing your home—it almost happened to me and my brother when our mum died. But of course I wouldn't expect *you* to give a damn about a thing like that—so long as you can make a profit on the deal, that's all you care about.'

'You don't seem to have a very high opinion of me,' he remarked drily.

'Well, you don't have a very high one of me!'

'No, I don't,' he conceded, his mouth taking on a cynical twist. 'And this latest performance isn't going to persuade me to change my mind. The tart with a heart—I'm afraid Hollywood has done that one to death.'

Lacey felt her anger boiling up, and resolutely clamped it down—she wasn't going to give him the satisfaction of letting him needle her. 'Oh, it's a waste of time trying to argue with you,' she snapped. 'I'm going to have a look around.'

She picked up the dusty old saucer that held the stub of candle and stalked off down the passage. So much for fantasies, she reflected bitterly; her dream cottage had turned out to be a damp, tumbledown ruin, and the man was positively hateful! She'd have been better off staying at home and facing the music.

The rest of the cottage seemed to be as dilapidated as the hall. The parlour didn't look as if it had been used for years, and neither did the dining-room—Miss Haversham herself would have felt quite at home among the festoons of dusty cobwebs.

'Ugh!' Lacey uttered, her nose wrinkling in distaste. 'I hope you didn't pay a lot for this place—you were done.'

'I bought it for the land,' he responded evenly. 'It adjoins a property I already owned, to make a substantial spread. The house was just incidental. And for your information,' he added, sensing her hostility, 'the owner was delighted to make the sale. He was well past the age when he wanted to retire, and he was having considerable difficulty finding a buyer—on its own, the place just wasn't economically viable. I gave him a very fair price for it, and he's now living very happily in a nice little bungalow in Scarborough, near his daughter.'

Lacey shrugged her slim shoulders in a gesture of obstinate indifference, and walked on down the passage, Khan trotting happily at her heels, thoroughly enjoying the adventure. The passage elbowed to the right, and she opened a door into what had clearly once been the most used room in the house—a cosy farmhouse kitchen.

'Ah, now this looks a little better,' she approved, holding up the candle to reveal a low, beamed ceiling and exactly the sort of inglenook fireplace she had envisaged, complete with an old-fashioned iron range. The floor was of cracked quarry tiles covered with an old patterned carpet, almost threadbare in places; against one wall stood a large Welsh dresser, and there was a scrubbed pine table in the middle of the room.

'If we can get that range alight, at least it should warm this room a little,' Jon remarked, nodding his head towards the range. 'We'd better sleep in here tonight—the rest of the house will probably be too cold and damp.'

'In . . . here?' Lacey's heart kicked abruptly against her chest. 'Both of us?'

'Of course.' A dark glint of humour lurked in the depths of his eyes. 'Don't worry, you'll be quite safe—I have no designs on your . . . er . . . virtue.'

Stupidly, his persistent contempt still stung, but she wasn't going to let him see that. Tilting up her chin, she regarded him with haughty disdain. 'Aren't you afraid I'll try to blackmail you, too?' she returned coldly. 'After all, you're giving me plenty of evidence, spending the night alone with me out here in the middle of nowhere, with only a batty old lady for a chaperon.'

A smile of lazy mockery curved that hard mouth. 'Oh, I don't think you'd dare try that,' he murmured, his voice smooth and dangerous. 'Would you?'

Those dark eyes had captured hers, and a chill of ice scudded down the length of her spine. She couldn't imagine anyone trying to blackmail Jon Parrish; beneath that urbane exterior was a streak of utter ruthlessness. But knowing that didn't help, she acknowledged with a hint of desperation; it only increased that powerful animal magnetism that drew her helplessly like a moth to a flame, even though she knew it would burn her wings to ashes.

With an effort of will she managed to break the spell and, turning away from him, walked over to the range, bending to open the door and peer inside. 'It...seems quite clean,' she managed, her voice shaking only slightly. 'What are we going to use for kindling? I doubt if there's any in stock.'

'We'll have to see if we can find some old bits of furniture to break up,' he suggested. 'I wouldn't mind betting there's woodworm in a lot of it anyway.'

Khan though it was enormous fun to help drag a couple of mattresses and a pile of bedclothes down from the bedrooms to the kitchen. They weren't as damp as Lacey had feared; a couple of hours beside the range would make them quite dry enough to sleep on.

An hour later, they had managed to build quite a decent pile of firewood—they had found some old chairs in one of the bedrooms which betrayed the tiny pinprick holes that were evidence of the presence of woodworm, and Jon had broken them up into pieces with an axe he had found hanging in the scullery.

Watching him in the flickering candlelight, working with his jacket off and his shirtsleeves rolled back to show strong, sun-bronzed forearms lightly scattered with dark hair, Lacey felt an odd little fluttering in the muscles of her stomach.

She was very sure that she didn't like him—he was the most arrogant, high-handed, ruthless man she had ever met. No, what she felt was rather more basic— an instinctive response that was as old as Eve, the vulnerability of a woman for a prime dominant male.

The problem was, she didn't quite know how to handle it—it was something she had never experienced before, at least not as powerfully as this. Oh, she had had plenty of boyfriends—she couldn't even begin to count them. But she had never wanted to get serious with any of them—though quite a few had wanted to get serious with her. She had enjoyed kissing and flirting, but anything more than that . . . no.

So why the hell did it have to be *this* man, who had already made it clear what he thought of her? Even though that one kiss was still seared into her brain, she knew there would be no repetition—he wasn't the sort of man who would lower himself to make love with a woman he believed had been having an affair with his own stepfather. And even if by some remote chance he let himself be tempted, it would only increase his contempt for her.

And anyway, what was she doing, thinking about making love with him? she chided herself sharply. It went against every principle she had grown up with. Though perhaps she wouldn't expect to be married first, she would certainly expect there to be a deep and mutual commitment—of the heart and the mind, as well as the body. And even she wasn't naïve enough to imagine there could ever be that between them.

With a resolute effort of will she steadied the ragged beating of her heart, and pinned a bright smile in place. 'The range should be hotting up nicely now,' she remarked. 'Shall I put the kettle on, and make a cup of tea?'

'Coffee would be better,' he responded, straightening and wiping the film of sweat from his forehead with the back of his hand.

'OK. Er... black, no sugar—right?'

'Right.'

He seemed faintly amused that she had remembered, and she wished she had pretended she hadn't. Turning away, she hurried back into the kitchen, and began to unpack the bags of groceries he had bought.

She had wondered what sort of selection he would pick for a vegetarian—some people had some pretty weird ideas—but he hadn't done too badly. There was spaghetti, and rice, and a good selection of fresh and tinned vegetables, as well as several cartons of long-life milk. Enough for a week ... Surely they wouldn't be staying here that long?

'How about something to eat?' she called out to him. 'I could rustle you up my very own version of vegetarian spaghetti bolognese.'

'Sounds intriguing,' he admitted, bringing another armful of chopped wood to stack beside the range.

She flickered a shy glance up at him. She had lit several more candles that she had found in a box in the dresser, and by their soft glow his face had lost some of its hard arrogance. Their light seemed to warm his eyes, bringing out flecks of gold—and when he smiled at her she felt her heart skitter.

'It...won't take me very long,' she managed, a slight tremour in her voice that she hoped he wouldn't notice. 'Why don't you sit down for a while? We've plenty of wood to be going on with.'

He accepted her suggestion, settling himself in an old rocking-chair beside the fireplace. Khan, who had been off exploring by himself, came padding in and settled himself contentedly at his feet, his head draped over his crossed ankles, heaving a deep sigh and apparently dropping straight off to sleep.

It was warm in the kitchen now, and Lacey thought for a moment that Jon was dozing too; but then she caught the glitter of his eyes beneath his lashes—long, silken lashes, almost like a girl's, quite out of place on that hard-boned face.

She bustled around, cooking the dinner, trying to pretend that she was indifferent to his presence. But it made her nervous to know that he was watching her—she never knew what he was thinking. Her hands were shaking slightly as she strained the spaghetti and dumped it on the plates.

'There. I'm ... afraid it's not much,' she apologised as she invited him to the table. 'It's a good job we had a decent lunch.'

He sat down and picked up his fork, trying a sample of the sauce. 'Mmm—that's good,' he approved, taking another forkful. 'You're not a bad cook.'

'Thank you,' she murmured, dimpling a smile as she sat down opposite him. 'My mother taught me.'

'When did you become vegetarian?'

'Oh, a few years ago. I saw a programme on television about an abattoir, and it turned me right off meat—all those poor animals.'

A flicker of something passed behind his eyes. 'What about your boyfriend?' he enquired. 'Does he eat meat?'

'I'm afraid so,' she responded, remembering in time that he was talking about Hugo. 'I've tried to persuade him, but he won't give it up. He's worried about his muscles.'

'He does weight-lifting?'

She shook her head. 'He works out with weights, but not for weight-lifting. He's... a sort of dancer—he's in a group with five other guys.' An irrepressible giggle rose to her lips. 'They're called *Les Sauvages*. They take their clothes off.'

He raised one dark eyebrow in astonishment. 'You mean he's a male stripper?'

'Well, not exactly,' she assured him quickly. 'They don't take everything off—it's a very clean act. And they're awfully popular. I've been to a few of his shows, and the girls absolutely love it. He started doing it while he was at college, to help pay his way, and... well, it's very good money.'

'I should imagine it is,' he responded drily. 'Good luck to him.'

She slanted him a searching look from beneath her lashes. What was he thinking? It would surely just have reinforced his opinion of her to find out that while she was supposedly cavorting with his step-father, she was living with a man who took his clothes off for a living.

Not that she cared, she told herself resolutely; in fact, the worse he thought of her the better. He was far too proud a man to lower himself to seduce the kind of tramp he had labelled her. And that was her strongest line of defence; because she had an uncomfortable feeling that if he chose to try it, she wouldn't know how to prevent him.

They finished their meal in a silence that was a little more comfortable than at lunch. Then Lacey found a Ludo board and some dice in the bottom of the dresser, and challenged Jon to a game. She was a little surprised when he readily accepted, but there really wasn't much else to do, with only candle-light to see by.

The evening ticked away quietly; the only sounds were the occasional crackling of the wood in the fire, or the odd noises Khan made as he dreamed of chasing rabbits.

'Oh, dear—I think you're going to beat me again.' Lacey surveyed the board with a wry grimace as she counted the score on the dice as Jon threw them. 'That's six times in a row. I think you must be cheating.'

He laughed, sweeping her piece off the board. 'How can you possibly cheat at Ludo?'

'I don't know—but I'm sure if there was a way you'd use it.'

'What a terrible opinion you have of me!' he protested. 'I can assure you, I've never cheated in my life.'

'Never?' she queried, lifting one finely arched eyebrow in playful disbelief. 'That would make you a saint.'

He slanted her a look of teasing challenge. 'How do you know I'm not?'

Her heart kicked sharply against her ribs. Somehow, in the humid warmth of this farmhouse kitchen, by the soft glow of the candles, that icy reserve of his seemed to have melted somewhat. But the change had rendered him even more dangerous—and suddenly she was finding it difficult to breathe.

'Shall I ... put the kettle on again?' she suggested a little unsteadily. 'I fancy another cup of tea before we ... before it's time for ... bed.' The last word came out rather strangled, and she felt her cheeks flush a heated red. To cover it, she rose quickly to her feet and went to fill the kettle.

Jon laughed softly. 'Nervous of spending the night in here with me?' he taunted.

'Of course not.' It took a considerable effort to suppress the nervous tremor in her voice. 'You promised me you have no designs on my virtue.'

A dark flame flickered in his eyes, and he smiled with sardonic amusement. 'That's right,' he conceded. 'You couldn't be safer.' He rose lazily to his feet. 'I'd better go and fetch another couple of those chairs down,' he remarked. 'We need to make sure we've got enough wood to keep the range going until morning.'

Khan followed him devotedly from the kitchen, and with a small sigh Lacey packed away the Ludo pieces into their box, and bent to put them back in the cupboard. In spite of his assurance there was a small knot of apprehension curling in her stomach; it was going to be a long night.

She heard Jon's footsteps coming down the stairs; and then suddenly there was a shout, and the sound of something falling. With a gasp of horror she ran out into the hall. Jon was sprawled awkwardly at the foot of the stairs, all tangled up with Khan and two of the old chairs.

CHAPTER FIVE

'Oh, my goodness! Are you all right?' Lacey cried, running to help him.

Jon sat up, his expression grim. 'That damned dog...! He got right under my feet. No, get off me, you mobile hearthrug! I don't want my face washed.'

Khan, who had been enthusiastically licking his face under the mistaken impression that this constituted an apology, promptly redoubled his efforts, until Lacey was forced to drag him off—he had caused enough problems already, and she was afraid that this time Jon would be really angry with him.

'I'm really sorry,' she apologised awkwardly. 'Are you hurt?'

'I haven't broken anything,' he responded with terse impatience. He heaved himself to his feet. 'Fortunately I was only a couple of steps...' He broke off, his face twisting in pain as he tried to put his foot to the floor.

'You *are* hurt!' She took his arm solicitously. 'Quickly, sit down. Is it bad? Is it broken?'

'No, it isn't broken,' he grated, shaking her off. 'It's just a sprain. Help me into the kitchen.'

He gritted his teeth, leaning his weight on her shoulder. She helped him to a chair, and then knelt quickly to ease his shoe and sock off as gently as she could, appalled to see that the ankle was already swelling and very red.

'It looks nasty. I'd better put a cold bandage on it—that should help it a bit. It's all right—I know what I'm doing,' she added, lifting earnest violet eyes to his. 'I've done a first-aid course.'

'All right, then,' he grumbled irritably. 'Get on with it.'

His harsh tone cut her, but, having sprained her ankle once herself, Lacey knew just how painful it could be. She hurried off to find an old sheet to tear up for strips of bandage, trying not to let herself feel hurt at his ungracious manner—she was accustomed to that from dealing with Hugo; strong men always seemed to make the very worst patients.

To her relief, Khan at least seemed to have been forgiven; she returned to the kitchen to find him sitting quietly, his head in Jon's lap, gazing up at him in pure adoration—he seemed to understand that it was not the moment to be boisterous.

She worked quickly, using her teeth to start a nick in the worn cotton so that she could rip it down the thread, and soaking the strips in a bowl of cold water. When she had enough, she went back to Jon's chair and knelt on the floor again, lifting his foot tenderly into her lap.

'Ready?' she asked, glancing up at him. 'I'll try not to hurt you.'

He nodded, a slightly odd expression in his eyes that she couldn't quite read. She bent her head, concentrating all her attention on wrapping the bandage tightly around his poor ankle, now so badly swollen that tears of sympathy rose to her eyes. It was a very nasty sprain—he wasn't going to be able to put any weight on it for several days.

At last she finished the bandaging, tying it off neatly with a secure knot and tucking the ends in. 'There,' she breathed, smiling up at him. 'Is that better?'

'Much better, thank you.'

His voice had lost that rough edge, and in the soft glow of the candles his eyes gleamed with a warm light, as if the slow-burning embers of some primeval fire were kindled in their depths. As she gazed up into them, she felt as if she were being held by some strange, mesmeric power that she didn't know how to evade...

He put out his hand, and stroked it gently down over her golden hair. 'You know, you really are a very beautiful girl,' he murmured, his voice taking on a husky timbre. 'It's easy to understand why so many men would want you...'

He had moved his foot from her lap and, bending forward, wrapped both hands into her hair, drawing her up to her knees. And as she gazed up at him, she seemed to have forgotten to breathe, caught up in a mysterious spell that had somehow brought all her fantasies to life.

He tilted up her face, his lips warm as they brushed over hers, the hot tip of his tongue languorously tracing their soft shape. 'And you taste so sweet,' he growled hungrily. 'Like wine and honey...'

She was helpless to resist the plundering invasion of his kiss. His tongue swept deep into the moist, defenceless valley of her mouth, exploring every secret, sensitive corner with a flagrant sensuality that left her dazed, dizzy from the racing swirl of the blood in her veins, drugged by the heady muskiness of his skin.

Smoky shadows floated in her brain. She had lost all consciousness of where she was, or why—she probably couldn't even have remembered her own name. Time ceased to have any meaning; past and future, and all else beyond the bounds of this magical embrace, had melted away...

When he finally let her go she could only stare up at him through misted eyes, unable to conceal any of the emotions that were swirling inside her. And then he laughed, a chillingly cynical laugh that mocked her innocent vulnerability.

'You're quite an actress,' he taunted. 'If I hadn't known you better, I could almost have thought that little performance was genuine.'

His words were like a dousing of cold water, extinguishing all her silly romantic dreams at one cruel blow. But some part of her mind was still clinging to the ragged shreds of her pride; at least if he believed she had been acting, she could still salvage a small crumb of dignity. She slanted him a deliberately provocative glance from beneath her lashes as she picked up the remains of the bandages, and rose to her feet.

'I'm glad you enjoyed it,' she purred seductively. 'It certainly took your mind off your bad ankle for a few minutes, didn't it?'

He accepted that with a laugh. 'You know, for once I think my stepfather showed remarkably good taste,' he mused. 'You're quite a girl.'

Somehow she managed to keep her smile in place, though it felt as though her face had been set in plaster of Paris. If he still believed she had been having an affair with his stepfather, even after a kiss like that, she was never going to be able to convince him.

'I'll put the kettle on,' she suggested lightly. 'I could certainly do with that cup of tea now.'

Lacey didn't expect to sleep a wink, knowing that Jon was so close beside her, but after having so little sleep the previous night, and all the dramas of the day, she slept like a log, snuggled beneath a pile of blankets, with the old range giving off a steady glow of warmth all night and Khan curled up against the back of her knees as usual.

It was Khan who woke her, snuffling his cold wet nose into her ear as the first grey light of morning crept into the sky. A glance at her watch told her that it was almost seven o'clock, and with a yawn she sat up, wrapping the blankets around her shoulders.

Jon appeared to be still fast asleep; she could hear the deep, even sound of his breathing, and see the top of his dark head, turned away from her. Careful not to wake him, she slipped out of bed, and crept into the scullery to have a quick wash. Then, warmly dressed in a pair of jeans and a thick hand-knitted sweater, with her vast raincoat wrapped almost twice around her waist, she slipped Khan's lead on, and ventured out into the cold early morning.

The fog of last night had cleared away and the sight that met her eyes made her stop and draw in her breath. The house was set at the head of a broad, gentle valley, ringed by hills that were ancient long before the Ice Ages had shaped their present contours. The landscape was wild and empty beneath a pale winter sky, and the hard ground was touched white with frost that turned every tree and hedgerow to fine lace.

'How about this then, Khan?' she queried with delight. 'No place for a coward soul—or is that the Yorkshire moors? No matter—it could just as easily be here.'

They set off down the lane to explore. Lacey was soon wishing she knew a little about birds; there were flocks of them, scratching for worms in the ploughed fields or singing in the branches of the trees—she thought she recognised a chaffinch, but she wasn't sure, and there was some kind of hawk, with black tips to its wings, hovering in the sky. Khan found a late hedgehog bumbling along, looking for a drier place to sleep; he had never seen one before, and couldn't understand why it didn't want to make friends.

At last she turned back, her stomach prompting her to think about breakfast. The farmhouse looked a lot better in daylight. True, the cobbled yard was uneven and badly overgrown, and the ivy tangling the walls would need to be tackled, but with a little attention it could be charming.

The old caravan, lurching drunkenly on its bricks in the corner of the yard, could have been abandoned; all the windows were covered with cardboard on the inside, and the weeds had grown up around it. But as she passed it on her way back from her walk she sensed a movement, and noticed one corner of the cardboard at the side window twitch.

She hesitated, wondering if she would be greeted with a smile or the shotgun this morning, but decided to take the chance anyway. 'Good morning, Mrs Dinsdale,' she called cheerfully.

The door opened, and a grey head appeared, peering out at her with lingering suspicion. 'Huh?'

'It's a lovely day,' Lacey went on, injecting as much friendliness as she could into her tone. 'All the fog's gone.'

The door opened a little wider. 'Aye—it wouldn't last long. You're up very early this morning.'

'I was taking the dog for a walk,' Lacey explained. 'Just down the lane. He found a hedgehog, but he didn't know what it was—he's never seen one before.'

Khan had darted forward, and the old housekeeper bent to stroke his scruffy head. 'It's good to have a dog around the place again,' she chuckled. 'They give it a bit of life.' She opened the caravan door wide. 'Come on inside and sit a while,' she invited. 'I've got the kettle on, and a nice bit of stotty-cake if you want it.'

Lacey restrained her astonishment at this welcome. 'Thank you,' she responded warmly. 'I'd love it.'

To her surprise, the caravan was spotless inside, though crammed with what were evidently the keepsakes of a lifetime. Mrs Dinsdale went round to all the windows, pulling down the cardboard and folding it neatly to stow it away under the cushions of the built-in seats.

'There, that's better,' she approved, straightening the bright flowered curtains. 'I put that up to keep the warmth in at night—it gets a bit chilly, and the Calor runs up expensive.'

'Yes, I expect it does,' Lacey concurred, smiling. 'What a lot of lovely ornaments you have.'

The housekeeper beamed with delight. 'Some of them were old Mr Edward's—he couldn't take all of them when he moved near his daughter. This here's Staffordshire.' She picked up a heavy model of a horse. 'A Shire horse, it is. They used to have them on all the farms around here when I was a lass, but you don't see many of them these days—it's all tractors now.'

'It's very nice.' Lacey put out her hand and touched the cool china.

'You can't really show them off properly in here,' the old lady sighed, gazing sadly around her tiny home. 'There isn't enough room. They need a nice cabinet.'

Lacey felt her heart twist in sympathy—and anger at the man still probably fast asleep in the warm farmhouse kitchen. Well, he needn't think he was going to get away with evicting a defenceless old woman—that *would* make a story for the newspapers!

Mrs Dinsdale lumbered down to the compact little kitchen at the far end of the caravan, where a kettle was singing merrily on the hob. 'Now, let's see about this tea,' she mumbled, mostly to herself, reaching up a creaking arm to take a painted tin tea-caddy from the cupboard and count out three spoonfuls into a round brown teapot. 'One for you, one for me, and one for the pot.'

'Can I give you a hand?' Lacey offered, starting to her feet.

'No, no, love—I can manage. Now, here's the sugar and the milk. I always use this little jug—it was Mr Edward's favourite.'

The tea, when it was poured, was thick and brown, with a couple of stray tealeaves floating on the top;

Lacey had to force herself to smile as she sipped it. 'Delicious!'

'Good. Drink it up—there's plenty more in the pot...'

Suddenly Khan, who had been lying happily on the floor, bounced up, barking. Lacey glanced out of the window, and was shocked to see two cars, one a police car, driving slowly down the lane. Her first thought was that her whereabouts had somehow been discovered, and she shrank back, hiding behind the curtains.

But Mrs Dinsdale was instantly on her feet, transformed from the kindly old lady serving tea. Opening a cupboard, she took out the shotgun, her arthritic old fingers fumbling to load it with cartridges. 'I told them,' she was muttering fiercely, 'I'm not going off this place...'

'Mrs Dinsdale?' The two cars had parked across the entrance to the farmyard, and one of the policemen had got out and was walking cautiously towards the caravan. 'Hello?'

As Lacey watched, aghast, the old lady opened one of the windows just enough to poke the barrel of the shotgun out. 'Get back!' she shouted. 'I'm warning you...'

'Now, come on, Edna, you know this isn't going to do any good,' the policeman tried coaxingly. 'They've got a legal notice of eviction——'

'Get back!' Her voice was rising close to hysteria. 'I don't care what legal notice they've got. This here's my home—has been since before any of you was born, and you're not throwing me off it.'

'Now don't be silly——'

She cocked the gun. 'Get back or I'll fire.'

Lacey jumped quickly to her feet. 'Wait!' she gasped, a sudden thought striking her. 'Wait a minute.' She darted out of the door, leaving Khan shut inside, and waved the policeman back. 'Stay there,' she pleaded. 'I won't be a minute.'

She ran across the yard into the farmhouse, and down the passage. To her relief, Jon was up and dressed, sitting at the wooden table eating a spartan breakfast of bread and butter. He glanced up in surprise as she rushed in.

'The police are here with the bailiffs to evict Mrs Dinsdale,' she announced breathlessly. 'Come and tell them to go away.'

'I beg your pardon...?'

'Tell them to go away,' she repeated impatiently. 'You own this place—you can stop them evicting her. Tell them you've changed your mind.'

He shook his head, frowning. 'Wait a minute...'

She confronted him with her hands on her hips, her eyes sparking with fury. 'The *police* are here,' she emphasised. 'And she's got her shotgun out. This is her home—you've got no right to throw her out of it. What does it mean to you, this place?' She waved her hand around in a gesture that encompassed the general state of neglect. 'Nothing. If you don't come outside right now and sort it out...'

He held up his hand, conceding defeat. 'All right, all right—I'm coming.' He rose awkwardly to his feet. 'I could do with a stick or something...'

'There's a walking stick in the hall!' she remembered, darting out to fetch it.

She hovered solicitously at his side as he limped heavily down the passage. In spite of his crumpled shirt and his uncombed hair, and the dark shadow of beard on his jaw, he still carried that air of effortless authority. With a few crisp words he had convinced both the police and the bailiffs of who he was, and invited them into the farmhouse to discuss the situation.

Lacey hastened over to the caravan, and tapped on the door. 'It's all right, it's only me,' she called reassuringly.

The door opened cautiously, and Mrs Dinsdale peered out, her old eyes narrowed with suspicion as she peered around the yard.

'They've gone into the house,' Lacey told her. 'Don't worry, it's all going to be sorted out. I'll explain later. Please, don't do anything silly.'

The housekeeper's face was furrowed by a puzzled frown, but she nodded, and closed the door.

As she darted back across the yard, Lacy was a little surprised to see a youngish man in a leather aviator-style jacket peering into Jon's car—presumably he was the bailiff's assistant. He glanced up, smiling, as she passed. 'Hello. What's going on?' he asked.

'Oh, they won't be long,' she told him, feeling sorry for him at being left to kick his heels out here while the others were in the warm kitchen. 'Jon will probably have to ring his lawyers and tell them to stop the eviction proceedings, and then Mrs Dinsdale can stay.'

'Jon?'

She nodded. 'He owns the company that bought the farm from Mr Grainger.'

An odd look came into his eyes. 'You mean Jon Parrish?' he queried carefully. '*He's* here?'

'Yes.' She smiled, amused that he should be so impressed. 'That's his car.'

'And ... you're his secretary, are you?' the young man enquired.

'Er ... no.' Suddenly she was wary. Why should he be asking her that? An uncomfortable suspicion was forming in her brain. 'Well, I ... I'll be seeing you ...'

'Wait a minute ...'

But she darted into the house and closed the door behind her, leaning against it and closing her eyes. Damn—what an *idiot* she was! She ought to be able to spot a reporter at twenty paces by now. And after going to all this trouble to get away from them ... !

But maybe it would be all right, she told herself optimistically. He hadn't recognised her, at least— maybe he hadn't made the connection between her and Jon. His interest in Jon was probably just because he owned a lot of land in the area, and even if it was mentioned in the local paper that he was here it was unlikely that the London papers would pick up the information. She hoped.

Drawing a deep, steadying breath to help compose herself, she walked down the passage to the kitchen. Jon was sitting at the large wooden table, with the bailiff and the two policemen; he was talking on his mobile phone, and he glanced up as she appeared, a glint of sardonic amusement in his dark eyes.

'OK, Richard, fax that through as soon as it's finished ... Yes, keep me informed on that one—I may be here for a while. Well, gentlemen,' he concluded, switching off the phone, 'I trust that settles every-thing? I'm sorry you've been troubled.'

'No trouble, sir—no trouble at all,' the bailiff in-sisted deferentially, rising to his feet. 'Very nice to have met you, miss,' he added with a polite nod towards Lacey.

She managed some kind of response, a little em-barrassed at the realisation that he couldn't have helped noticing the pile of bedding on the floor beside the range—and to make it worse, Jon had bundled everything together when he had got up, so that it appeared as if there had been only one bed.

The two policemen departed with the bailiff, leaving her alone with Jon again. He lifted one dark eyebrow in quizzical enquiry.

'Satisfied?'

She dimpled him a warm smile, putting any other thoughts out of her mind. 'Thank you. That was really a very nice thing to do.'

'I was under the impression I had a gun to my head—both metaphorically and literally,' he re-sponded with a trace of dry humour.

She laughed, shaking her head. 'Come over and see Mrs Dinsdale,' she urged. 'Honestly, you'll be really surprised at her caravan—it's as neat as a pin inside. She's really not batty at all, you know—I think it was just being stuck out here with no one to talk to, and worrying about losing her home, that was making her go a bit funny.'

He quirked a quizzical eyebrow towards her. 'You seem to have made friends with her in a remarkably short space of time.'

'She's a dear—and Khan loves her. And listen,' she added, her eyes bright, 'I've had a terrific idea. If you're going to turn this place into holiday flats, you'll need to have someone around to keep an eye on the place for you, make sure the visitors have everything they want and that they look after the place for you...'

'You're surely not suggesting that I should employ Mrs Dinsdale?' he protested.

'Why not? I don't think she's even all that old—she's probably only in her middle fifties, if that. She'd be perfect.'

He conceded a smile of wry humour. 'First you foist that dim-witted mutt on to me, now a housekeeper I'm not sure I need ... All right, let's go and see her—but I'm making no promises, mind.'

Lacey grinned in triumph. Somehow, sometime yesterday evening, the whole atmosphere had changed between them, and the improvement seemed to be continuing. She wasn't quite sure what had caused it, and she knew that she still had to be very careful—but she couldn't quite extinguish the little glow of warmth in her heart.

Lacey enjoyed housework; it gave her a sense of satisfaction to see windows shining and woodwork gleaming with polish, where hours earlier there had been thick dust and cobwebs. And the physical exertion was just what she needed; the thought of staying here for several more nights with Jon—even in separate bedrooms—was decidedly unnerving.

Mrs Dinsdale had come in to help her, and proved to have a remarkable degree of energy. Together they turned out two of the bedrooms, washing the grime from the windows and lighting fires in the grates to take the damp and chill out of the air.

'There!' remarked Lacey proudly as she arranged a few rather rainswept late roses in a jug on the mantelshelf in the room she had picked for herself. 'That's much better!'

'Yes,' the housekeeper nodded. 'It's nice to see the old place looking bonny again. Now then, would you like me to show you how to make pan hacklety for your supper?'

'What is it?' Lacey asked curiously.

'You take a bit of cheese, and some nice vegetables, and fry them all up together till they're piping hot. Then you can serve them up with a nice bit of bread.'

'Sounds good!'

'What does?' Jon enquired, meeting them at the top of the stairs. He had spent most of the day sawing up wood for the fires, an activity which, somewhat to Lacey's surprise, he had seemed to have thoroughly enjoyed. He had rolled his shirtsleeves right up, displaying a definition of muscle that even Hugo could have envied, and he hadn't shaved—his jaw was dark with a day's growth of beard. It lent him a faintly gypsyish air—no longer the smooth, urbane businessman she had first met.

'What I'm going to cook you for dinner,' she informed him, her eyes dancing merrily. 'But why don't we have a cup of tea first? I think we deserve it.'

He smiled at her—that smile that could make her heart turn over. 'You've certainly been busy—you've transformed the place.'

'*We've* transformed the place,' she corrected him, pointedly including Mrs Dinsdale in the praise.

Jon picked up the hint at once. 'Yes, of course,' he added to the housekeeper, turning to her with one of his most charming smiles. 'You've done wonders—thank you very much indeed.'

She sniffed, embarrassed at the compliment. 'Aye, well—I was glad of having something to do...'

A sudden loud thumping on the front door, accompanied by vociferous barking from Khan, took them all by surprise.

Lacey's eyes widened. 'Who on earth...?' The next moment two faces appeared at the window, and she caught a glimpse of a camera. 'Reporters!'

'Damn!' Jon moved swiftly to draw the curtains across the window, although he was still limping heavily. 'I didn't think they'd be on to us that quickly.'

Lacey put her hand to her mouth. 'I'm sorry,' she confessed. 'It's my fault. This morning... There was a man hanging around outside, looking at your car, and...I'm afraid I just didn't think. I thought he was with the bailiff, but then he started asking a lot of questions. I'd...mentioned your name before I realised—but I didn't tell him mine.'

Jon sighed wryly. 'You wouldn't have had to—after yesterday's little escapade the wires have probably been buzzing all over the country. Any journalist worth his salt would have been able to put two and two together. Presumably he was from the local rag?'

'You mean young Gordon Harbottle?' put in Mrs Dinsdale. 'Aye—the long-nosed young devil. Always poking around where he isn't wanted.'

'Quite. Well, now that the vanguard are here, I don't suppose it'll be long before the whole pack of them are down on us.'

'What are we going to do?' Lacey queried anxiously.

'Do?'

'Well, couldn't we try to shake them off, and find somewhere else to stay?'

He shook his head. 'Now that they've found us, it won't be so easy to give them the slip a second time. Besides, this ankle of mine's not up to much driving, and I'm afraid I'm not prepared to trust you with my car.'

'I can't drive anyway,' she retorted, as indignant at his attitude as if she had been able to. 'I've never been able to afford the money to take lessons.'

'Well, there you are, then,' he responded with a sardonic smile. 'Anyway, where could we have gone? I don't imagine it would be very easy to find a hotel that would be willing to risk their carpets and furniture—not to mention their other guests' sanity—to that delinquent hound of yours.'

Since her pet was at that moment giving a fair impression of homicidal insanity, gouging deep scratches out of the front door, Lacey felt she could hardly argue. 'So... We have to stay here then?' she queried apprehensively.

He shrugged his wide shoulders in a gesture of unconcern. 'I'm afraid so. We'll just have to make the best of it.'

Lacey wished she could feel so relaxed about the prospect; but the thought of being trapped here alone with him, unable even to get out of the house, was not one she could view with any degree of equanimity.

At least tonight they wouldn't have to sleep in the kitchen. Last night, knowing that he was so close, her dreams had been filled with disturbing images of those dark, dangerous eyes. She would feel at least a little safer—not so much from him as from herself—if there was a locked door between them.

CHAPTER SIX

'OH, this is getting crazier by the minute!' Lacey protested fretfully, tossing down the book she had been flicking through and going over to peer out of the bedroom window at the activity in the cobbled farmyard. 'There's a television crew arrived now, and they're taking pictures of the people trying to take pictures of us.'

Jon laughed drily. 'If you're going to stand there where they can see you, we might as well have stayed downstairs with the curtains open,' he pointed out.

'They can't see me from here,' she responded, stepping back to make sure of it. This whole situation was beginning to drag on her nerves; since last night they had been forced to close all the downstairs curtains against the prying eyes of the reporters with their cameras, and today they had spent most of their time upstairs to save the candles.

She hated having nothing to do. She had managed to while away most of the morning cleaning and dusting the bedrooms again, and after lunch she had spent an hour or so giving Khan's coat a really thorough brushing. But now she was at a loose end—it was too early even to think about dinner yet.

Jon, on the other hand, appeared to be quite untroubled by the situation. He had found himself a book on one of the dusty bookshelves in the parlour, and settled himself comfortably in an old high-winged armchair beside the fire in the main bedroom, his injured foot propped up on a low stool. He was wearing a pair of casual jeans and a black sweater, and his hard jaw was dark now with two days growth of beard. If he tried to walk into his City office like that, Lacey reflected with a trace of wry amusement, he'd probably be thrown out by the doorman.

She took another look out of the window at the reporters huddled below. It had been drizzling with rain on and off all morning; some of them had rigged a kind of wind-shelter, using a large sheet of blue plastic, but it couldn't be doing very much good. In spite of her irritation at their presence, she couldn't help but feel a little concern for them.

'They must be getting awfully cold out there,' she mused softly. 'Poor things—I wonder if they'd like some soup...?'

Jon quirked one eyebrow in quizzical amusement. 'You're feeling *sorry* for them?' he teased.

'Well...' She shrugged her slender shoulders in confusion. 'I suppose they're only doing their jobs. It can't be much fun for them.'

'It isn't much fun for us, either,' he pointed out with a touch of asperity.

'I know.' She slanted him a glance of wry apology as she sat down on the edge of the bed. 'I'm sorry—this is all my fault. If I hadn't been so stupid about that reporter yesterday they wouldn't have found us.'

'There's no point fretting about it now,' he remarked dismissively, turning a page of his book. 'At least we're comfortable—they're the ones outside in the cold.'

'Yes, but you can just imagine the sort of stories they're going to be publishing about us,' she persisted. *'Mistress runs off with lover's stepson.* And I bet they'll make it sound really sordid.'

'I don't think so,' he responded with casual unconcern. 'I've had my lawyers warn them of possible libel action.'

'Oh...' She might have known it—he wasn't the sort of man to leave anything to chance. She watched him covertly from beneath her lashes as she picked up the book she had been trying to read—a local guide-book. He looked the picture of contented domesticity, sitting there in front of the fire, a thick copy of Dickens open on his lap. It would be so easy to let herself imagine a life like that—of being able to glance up and see him there, every day...

But that was a dangerous illusion, she reminded herself firmly. This was not the real Jon Parrish—he was just making the most of his enforced holiday. She and the real Jon Parrish would never even have come into contact with each other if it hadn't been for the unfortunate chance of her meeting his stepfather, and the fateful consequences that had flowed from that.

And it would be most unwise to relax her guard. Though he had been scrupulously careful not to get too close to her since that first night, she could still sense it, that unmistakable spark of physical awareness in the air between them, the glint in his eyes whenever he looked at her.

He had made it abundantly clear that he had nothing but contempt for her, and she suspected that he had an equal contempt for himself for wanting her; but last night, in the kitchen, when they had played

Ludo again, somehow even that innocent pastime had been charged with dark undercurrents of tension. And when it had been time to go to bed she had been glad she had chosen herself a room as far as possible from his, one with a lock on the door. But how much longer could they go on like this . . . ?

A sudden commotion below caught her attention, and she ran back to the window. A sleek silver BMW had turned into the farmyard, and the press-pack had descended on it like wolves. 'Who on earth . . . ?' She leaned forward curiously. 'It's a woman—a blonde woman. I wonder who it is?'

Jon put down his book, and rose to his feet. 'I think I can guess. I'd better go and let her in.'

She turned to him in surprise. 'You were expecting someone?'

A strange expression flickered briefly across his face. 'In a way.'

Curiosity drew her after him, though she waited discreetly at the top of the stairs. He was still favouring his injured foot slightly as he walked down the dim passage to the front door. She watched as he slid back the sturdy bolts, and then held it with his weight as he opened it a few inches. Through the narrow gap, she saw a rush as the reporters surged forward; but the blonde ducked swiftly under Jon's arm, and he slammed the door in their faces, bolting it firmly again.

The new arrival was clearly not amused; her mouth was taut as she brushed down her pearl-grey mink jacket and smoothed her immaculate hair. 'Well, really!' she protested indignantly. 'I didn't expect it to be like this!'

'Hello, Barbara,' Jon greeted her, a hint of sardonic amusement in his voice. 'I'm sorry about the welcome committee—they've been with us since last night.' He slid an arm around her waist, and bent to kiss her cheek, but she put up a hand to fend him off, leaning away from him.

'Good heavens, Jon—when did you last have a shave?' she protested in disgust.

He laughed wryly, rubbing his hand over his jaw. 'I'm sorry—there's no electricity in the house, and I don't have a wet razor with me. Anyway, what brings you up here?'

Blue eyes like ice-chips regarded him coolly. 'When I have newspaper reporters ringing me up in the middle of the night, asking me if I'm aware that my fiancé is on his honeymoon with another woman, I think I have a right to know what's going on, don't you?' she enquired in glacial tones. 'Really, Jon, I can appreciate your need to sort out the unpleasant mess your stepfather had got himself into, but why you had to get involved with that...that *tart* yourself, I don't know—let alone go careering off all round the country with her.'

At the top of the stairs, Lacey stiffened. *Tart*, indeed! How dared she? She'd never even *met* her! And as for Jon... For some reason she didn't care to explore too deeply, she felt an odd little chill in the region of her heart. Not that she should have been surprised that in his way he should prove as duplicitous as his stepfather, kissing her the way he had when he was engaged to someone else—and not just once, but twice!

Well, damn the pair of them! She certainly wasn't going to skulk up here as if *she* had something to be ashamed of, she vowed, setting her shoulders squarely as she started down the stairs. Unfortunately, at that moment Khan, who had been off exploring the nether reaches of the house, came bounding into the hall, barking joyously—he had heard the sound of a new arrival, and was eager to welcome her.

Unfortunately Barbara misinterpreted his intentions, and with a shriek of horror retreated behind Jon. This puzzled the intelligent hound, who persisted in his attempts to offer the hand of friendship, getting his large dirty paws all over her expensive cashmere skirt.

Lacey raced down the stairs and grabbed her pet, dragging him back. 'I'm awfully sorry,' she apologised breathlessly. 'He doesn't mean any harm. He doesn't bite, honestly.'

She found herself being regarded by those frosty blue eyes as Barbara regained her poise. 'I should hope not. I happen not to like dogs. Please endeavor to keep him under proper control—otherwise he'll have to be shut up.'

Oh yes? You haven't wasted much time in starting to lay down the law, Lacey fumed silently. But not one trace of these angry thoughts was permitted to appear on her face—there were better ways to get her revenge on both of them. She glanced questioningly towards Jon, inviting an introduction.

He obliged with a taut smile. 'Lacey, this is Barbara Harrington. My fiancée.'

'Really?' she slanted him a look of teasing re-proach from beneath her lashes. 'You never told me you were engaged.'

She had the satisfaction of seeing the instant sus-picion in Barbara's sharp eyes, and the glint of anger in his. 'It was irrelevant,' he rapped impatiently.

She lifted one finely arched eyebrow at him, delib-erately misunderstanding, and turned a look of sym-pathy on the arctic Barbara. 'Irrelevant? Oh, dear...' She let it appear that she was trying not to laugh. 'I think I'd better take Khan out of the way. I'll tell you what, why don't you two go upstairs to the bedroom, and I'll make us all a nice pot of tea.'

As she hustled the reluctant pup around the corner of the passage, she heard the start of the explosion behind her.

'And what exactly was *that* supposed to mean?' Barbara demanded, her voice conveying an unmis-takable frost-warning.

Jon sighed. 'I'm sorry—look, come upstairs and I'll explain everything.'

'And why were they saying you were on your honeymoon?' she persisted sharply. 'How could they possibly have got hold of a ridiculous idea like that?'

'Ah—I think that would have been Mrs Dinsdale.'

'Mrs Dinsdale? Who's she? And why should she think you were on your honeymoon?'

'It's...a long story. Come upstairs and I'll tell you all about it,' he coaxed.

'Why upstairs? What's wrong with staying down here?'

'It's dark down here,' he explained evenly. 'We have to keep the curtains closed because of the Press nosing in through the windows.'

Lacey heard their footsteps on the stairs. 'I don't understand why you had to bring her up here yourself anyway,' Barbara's voice persisted on a note of indignation. 'Let alone stay here with her...'

She went into the kitchen, and closed the door carefully behind her—in fact it cost her a considerable effort to resist the temptation to slam it. Her small hands had curled into fists, and her face was twisted into a grimace of frustration and rage.

Over the past couple of days she had slowly been revising her opinion of Jon; that remote, forbidding façade seemed to have melted a little to show a slightly more human side to his nature—especially when he had acceded to her request to offer Mrs Dinsdale the chance to stay. But she had clearly been wrong—any man who could get himself engaged to *that* lump of ice couldn't have an ounce of human warmth in his body!

Of course, Barbara *was* beautiful, she was forced to acknowledge, however reluctantly. Everything about her discreetly hinted class, from her smoothly bobbed ash-blonde hair to her racehorse-slim figure— and her clothes weren't rags either.

Well, if that was the sort he liked, she conceded with a dismissive shrug—they were probably very well suited. If she could, she would have packed her things and left immediately. But unfortunately that was impossible—she was going to have to stick it out.

But she wasn't going to allow that hateful pair to patronise her, she vowed fiercely. She still had a few tricks up her sleeve.

She took her time about making the tea—she had to be sure she could maintain her composure completely, in the face of whatever arose. And besides, she needed to plan her strategy. By the time she went back upstairs, she felt about ready to face whatever confrontation was to come.

Her entrance was perfectly staged—she all but dropped a curtsy. 'I've brought the tea,' she announced in her best housemaid's voice.

'Thank you.' Barbara had clearly walked the audition for the role of lady of the manor. 'Put it down here.' With an aristocratic gesture she indicated the small table which had been moved next to the armchair where she was sitting.

Lacey carried the tray across the room, acutely aware of Jon's eyes following her. He was leaning casually against the fireplace; he had removed that disreputable sweater, she noticed—no doubt at Barbara's insistence. But at least he couldn't have a shave; that two days' growth of stubble lent him a rakish air which she found extremely attractive, even if Barbara didn't.

'I didn't put sugar in—I hope that's right?' she queried deferentially.

'Yes, thank you,' came the haughty response.

'Oh, good—I thought you probably wouldn't take it.' She smiled in trusting confidence. 'Do you use artificial sweeteners?'

'No, I don't!' Barbara snapped, sweeping her a look of icy indignation.

Lacey allowed herself to look hurt, aware that Jon was watching her through eyes narrowed with suspicion. Well, let him wonder what she was up to; if nothing else, he was going to see Barbara in her true colours—and if he still wanted to marry her then, he would deserve all he got!

He glanced at the tray, noticing that there were only two cups. 'Aren't you having any tea?' he asked her sharply.

'Oh... No.' She slid him a lingering look, accompanied by a wistful little smile. 'I... don't want to be in the way. I'll have mine downstairs.'

'Bring it up here,' he insisted tersely. 'We need to talk.'

She lowered her eyes, humbly obedient. 'Yes, Jon,' she murmured, and slipped out of the room.

He came after her, ushering her down the stairs ahead of him, his grim expression unnerving her a little. He didn't speak until they got to the kitchen; then he closed the door firmly, his anger crackling in the air like electricity. 'All right—what was that all about?' he demanded.

Her violet-blue eyes held only limpid innocence. 'What was what all about?'

'You know, damn you!' He looked for a moment as if he wanted to shake her, but instead flung himself across the room, putting the table between them. 'You played that like a scene from some third-rate play. Are you trying to make Barbara look a fool?'

'I wouldn't dream of it,' she protested sweetly. 'I was only trying to be polite.'

He glared at her in warning fury. 'Well, just drop it.'

'You want me to be rude to her?' she queried, suitably bewildered.

'I want you to be...pleasant to her,' he ground out. 'Is that too much to ask?'

Yes it is, actually, she wanted to bite back. But with an effort of will she managed to keep up her cool façade, and instead shrugged her slender shoulders in a gesture of casual unconcern. 'I'll try,' she promised dubiously. 'Funny how you forgot to mention her, though.'

'I told you, my private life is none of your business.'

'No? Don't you think I'm entitled to know if a man's engaged when he's going to kiss me the way you did?' she accused bitterly.

His hard mouth curved into a humourless smile. 'I'm sorry,' he mocked on a note of jaded cynicism. 'I had no idea you had such scruples.'

'You still think I was having an affair with your stepfather?' she demanded, her voice ragged with frustration. Stupid tears were stinging at the backs of her eyes, and she turned her back on him to pick up the dishcloth and aimlessly wipe down the draining board. 'Oh... What the hell! Think whatever you like!'

He moved swiftly across the room, catching her arm in a vice-like grip and spinning her round to face him. 'Damn you—I don't know what to think any more,' he grated with sudden fierce intensity. 'You're like a chameleon—one minute as sweet and innocent as a kitten, the next a wanton little cat. You're driving me crazy...'

She stared up at him, her heartbeat accelerating alarmingly. Since Barbara had arrived, and she had discovered that he was engaged, she had been telling herself that the powerful forces she had sensed between them could be no more than an illusion. But the way he was looking at her now...

A sudden commotion outside the back door broke the strange spell. 'Get away with you, you bunch of great useless, worthless louts,' the housekeeper's unmistakable tones sounded at the back door. 'Before I take my broom to the lot of you!'

With a thud of relief, Lacey seized on the distraction, scooting over to unlock the door, careful to keep behind it. The ample lady was indeed wielding a large besom broom, which she was using to good effect to keep the Press reporters back out of her way as she stepped through the door.

Lacey closed and bolted the door swiftly, much impressed by the old lady's fortitude. 'Hello,' she greeted her warmly. 'You're just in time—I've just made a pot of tea.'

Mrs Dinsdale beamed at her comfortably. 'Yes, I won't say no, though I've not long had one,' she admitted, settling herself down at the table. 'But there's no harm going to come to you from a nice pot of tea, I always say.'

Lacey went to the dresser to fetch another cup and saucer, slanting Jon an uncertain glance as she stepped past him. The look he returned her told her she hadn't been mistaken, and she felt a hot flush of pink rise to her cheeks. He might be engaged to Barbara, but clearly he didn't regard that as any bar to indulging himself in a little dalliance on the side. And why should he? After all, he was only following his stepfather's example, she mused bitterly.

He turned back to the housekeeper, greeting her with impeccable politeness. 'Good morning, Edna. I hope our friends outside didn't cause you too much trouble?'

'Oh, them . . .' She lapsed into a mumbling tirade in broad Northumberland dialect. 'I wouldn't let them stop my way if I wanted to get through.'

He laughed. 'I'd certainly have to back you against them if it came to——'

'Ah—I see that you've decided to forgather in the kitchen after all,' Barbara's frigid tones cut in. 'How very cosy.' She cast a disparaging eye around the room, passing over Mrs Dinsdale as if she were no more than a stick of furniture.

That good lady, however, was not so easily ignored. 'And who might you be?' she demanded with all the blunt self-assurance of one who believed herself the rightful incumbent of the premises, entitled to welcome or refuse whomsoever she chose.

Barbara glanced back at her, lifting one finely-pencilled eyebrow in haughty surprise. 'I'm Mr Parrish's fiancée,' she responded, equally imperious.

Mrs Dinsdale looked shocked, turning a disapproving glare on Jon, as if she expected him to have suddenly sprouted a blue beard. 'Fiancée? You told me you were on your honeymoon,' she accused.

'I'm afraid you were mistaken,' Barbara cut in coldly.

'I'm sorry, Edna,' Jon apologised to the elderly housekeeper with a wry smile. 'When we first arrived it seemed easier to tell you that than to go into a long explanation about why we were really here. But as you know now, we were trying to get away from the Press...'

The old lady pursed her lips, clearly not impressed. 'Well, all I can say is I never knew such goings on,' she declared indignantly. 'If that's the sort of thing I can expect, I don't think I shall want to work for you after all, thank you very much.'

'Work for him?' Barbara queried sharply.

'Mrs Dinsdale is the housekeeper,' Lacey explained with some satisfaction.

'Housekeeper?' Barbara looked frankly incredulous. 'I thought you were planning to convert this place into holiday flats, Jon? Why should you need a housekeeper?'

'I think I might make some minor changes to the original plans,' he responded evenly. 'A lot of people want more than self-catering these days.'

Barbara frowned. 'But is that enough to make it economically viable to keep a housekeeper on?' she queried, coolly businesslike. 'I mean it would be different if she was...able to be a little more versatile.'

Lacey felt her jaw clench in anger; Barbara had been going to say 'younger', and dressing it up in fancy language didn't alter her meaning. It wasn't very often that she took a real dislike to someone, but from the minute she had heard that autocratic voice she had known that this young lady was trouble.

A sudden commotion from upstairs made them all look up; a scrabbling of paws, a fierce growling, and an odd banging noise. 'Khan!' Lacey cried. 'Someone's trying to get in through the window!'

She raced for the stairs, but Jon was already ahead of her. But as she reached the upper landing, she realised it wasn't an intruder her intelligent pet had been attacking—it was Barbara's expensive mink jacket. He had it by the sleeve, shaking it savagely, his paws well tangled in the ripped lining.

'My jacket!' shrieked Barbara. 'Oh—get it off him!'

The noble hound glanced up, proudly guarding his kill. As Jon approached, he backed away warily, dragging it with him, for the first time a little uncertain that his magnificent hunting prowess was meeting with universal approval.

'Drop it,' Jon commanded.

With instant obedience, it was laid at his feet; the voice of the leader of the pack was unmistakable, and Khan wasn't fool enough to risk a challenge. His tail wagging in hopeful propitiation, he fawned at the master's feet.

Jon picked up the tattered jacket, and examined it wryly. 'I'm afraid it's torn,' he remarked, holding it out to Barbara.

She snatched it from him, her eyes sparking with cold fury. 'It's ruined!' she protested, her voice rising on the verge of hysteria. 'Look at it!' She turned on Lacey. 'I told you to keep that dog under proper control.'

'It was you who let him out of the kitchen,' Lacey pointed out tautly.

'You'll replace it, of course,' Barbara grated, shaking it at her. 'I shall sue.'

Lacey shrugged, her own temper determinedly leashed. 'I don't have any money, and you can't get blood out of a stone,' she responded flippantly.

'Anyway, you can't blame him—he probably thought it was a rat.'

'A *rat* . . . ?'

Jon was obliged to step in before the quarrel escalated into physical violence. 'Why don't we finish our tea?' he suggested to Barbara, taking her arm in a grip from which she wasn't going to escape. 'Lacey, perhaps you'd better make sure Khan stays in the kitchen.'

Lacey returned him a look of angry resentment, but said nothing, taking a puzzled and rather sulky Khan by his collar and coaxing him down the stairs. He instantly forgot his disgrace when he found Mrs Dinsdale in the kitchen, bouncing over to welcome her excitedly.

'What was all that about?' the housekeeper asked with mild curiosity, nodding her head towards the stairs.

Lacey laughed with impish satisfaction. 'He'd got hold of Barbara's mink, and was busy killing it,' she explained.

'Mink? Huh!' Mrs Dinsdale expressed her opinion of the fabulously expensive jacket with a disapproving shrug. 'Fancy clothes are all very well, but fancy clothes don't make a fine lady. And you don't want to let her be staying here, you know—she'll just cause trouble.'

Lacey smiled wryly, sitting down on the opposite side of the table. 'Unfortunately I can't get rid of her that easily,' she sighed. 'She *is* Jon's fiancée, you see.'

Mrs Dinsdale frowned. 'Well, I don't expect to understand what's going on. All those nosy tykes out there peeking in through the windows... I don't know what people want to read the newspapers for anyway, just poking into other people's business as don't concern them. Pity they don't have anything better to do.' She finished her tea, and set down the cup. 'Well, I can't be sitting here all day,' she declared decisively, rising to her feet. 'I'm taking a walk down to the village, so I dropped by to see if you want anything from the shop, seeing as you can't get out of the house for all them nosy parkers around the door.'

'Oh—yes! Thank you.' The supplies Jon had bought were already running low, and with a third person now to feed it could soon become a problem. 'Could you get me some eggs, and some milk . . . ? I'd better make a list.'

An hour or so later, Jon came downstairs to find Lacey vigorously polishing the sideboard in the parlour. She had lit a fire in the grate, and it had drawn well, filling the room with a flickering orange glow, and she had rearranged the furniture, drawing it in around the fire, making the atmosphere seem altogether more snug.

He came into the room, and closed the door behind him. 'What are you doing?' he asked.

She slanted him a sardonic look. 'I just thought I'd tidy up in here a bit—I'm sure your fiancée won't want to stay upstairs all evening, and you can hardly expect her to sit in the kitchen.'

A spark lit his eyes as her words conjured, for both of them, a memory of the cosy times they had spent playing Ludo in the warmth of the range. Had that been her intention? She didn't even know herself any more.

He moved towards her. 'You were right,' he murmured softly. 'I should have told you about Barbara.'

It cost her some effort, but she carried on polishing, merely shrugging her slender shoulders in a gesture of indifference. 'It doesn't matter—as you said, it really wasn't any of my business.'

'But you're upset.'

'Of course I'm not,' she insisted, knowing that the slight waver in her voice was betraying the turmoil of emotions she didn't know how to control.

'No?' That firm, intriguing mouth had twisted into a wry smile. 'This whole thing has got a lot more complicated than I anticipated,' he admitted. '*You're* a lot more complicated than I anticipated.'

'Am I?' She couldn't keep the angry bitterness from her voice. 'I thought I was just the tart who was having an affair with your stepfather.'

He frowned, shaking his head. 'I don't know. Is that what you are? You're an actress—you could make yourself appear to be anything you choose.' He came towards her, those deep, mesmerising eyes holding hers so that she found herself unable to back away from him. 'The first time I met you, you seemed exactly the type—perhaps too much so. Did I jump to conclusions too quickly? Were you letting me tangle myself up in my own arrogant assumptions? Or are you fooling me now with those innocent blue eyes?'

As she gazed up at him, he put out his hand, and stroked his fingers back lightly along the line of her jaw, his thumb brushing across the delicate shell of her ear.

'I don't want to touch you, but I can't help myself,' he grated, his voice taut and husky. 'It sickens me to think of you with my stepfather, but when you look at me the way you do you can make me forget all about that—you can make me forget my own name.'

Her mouth was dry, and unconsciously she drew in a deep, ragged breath, making her chest rise and fall. His gaze dropped automatically to the full roundness of her breasts beneath the soft knit of her sweater, and she knew that her tender nipples had ripened to visible nubs, as if in deliberate invitation.

She saw his jaw tense, his eyes flicker with primitive desire. A momentary panic caught at her as she realised the danger, but it was too late to escape. His hand tangled into her hair, holding her prisoner, and his mouth descended on hers with a fierce hunger, crushing her lips apart.

But she could only surrender, betrayed by her own aching needs. His tongue was plundering deep into her mouth in a flagrantly sensual exploration, and he had pinned her back against the sideboard so that every inch of her body was curved helplessly against his. She knew that she was only reinforcing his most negative opinion of her, but she could do nothing about it; all her responses were spiraling out of control.

His mouth broke from hers, but only to dust scalding kisses across her trembling eyelids and the thundering pulse beneath her temple. The hot, moist tip of his tongue circled into the delicate shell of her ear, making her shiver with torrid heat, and went on to trace a path of fire down the exposed, vulnerable column of her throat to linger in the sensitive hollows of her shoulder, as his hand slid insistently up beneath her sweater to mould over the ripe swell of her breast, crushed tautly into the lacy cup of her bra.

For a moment he lifted his head, his eyes glittering down into hers. 'My God, I can't believe how much I want you, Lacey,' he grated. 'You're more than flesh and blood can resist.'

With an abrupt movement he released the catch of her bra, freeing the constrained fullness for his hands to enjoy. A small sob escaped her lips as her head fell dizzily back; he was caressing the silken warmth of her flesh with a devastating expertise, his clever fingers nipping at the exquisitely sensitive buds of her nipples, sending sparks of fire into her brain.

But some corner of her mind had managed to hold onto a shred of sanity, and with an effort of will she struggled to push him away. 'No,' she pleaded desperately. 'Stop...'

'Why?' he demanded savagely. 'You want this as much as I do.'

With a rush of shame she knew that she couldn't deny it. Her whole body was awash with exquisite sensation, and she felt as if her bones were melting. But still she struggled to resist the treacherous weakness that was urging her to surrender. 'You're engaged to Barbara,' she reminded him, turning her head aside to evade the insatiable demand of his lips.

A spark of anger flared in his eyes. 'I don't give a damn,' he growled, and pushing her sweater up to her throat he bent her back across the sideboard, burying his face between her ripe, flushed breasts, taking one succulent nipple into his mouth to suckle it with a deep, hungry rhythm.

She was losing the fight, drowning in a honeyed tide of feminine submissiveness. But she knew that if she gave in to him he would think nothing of her, and the one thing she couldn't bear was to see the contempt in his eyes, and know that it was deserved. Exerting every ounce of will-power she possessed, she pushed him away, the drag of his mouth on her breast as he refused to give her up almost fatally undermining her resistance.

'Leave me alone,' she hissed forcefully. 'I'm not going to sleep with you.'

'Why not?' he demanded, bitterly mocking. 'I'm a lot richer than my stepfather, you know—I can set you up in luxury, buy you anything you want. And I'm younger, and much more energetic—I could make love to you all night, every night. You'll never need anyone else.'

'Before or after you marry Barbara?' she protested, bitter humiliation stinging her heart.

'My marriage will alter nothing,' he asserted with cynical conviction. 'Wives and mistresses are quite separate things—they each serve a different function in life. And while Barbara possesses all the attributes I require in a wife, you, my sweet Lacey, were eminently created to be a mistress.'

'No...' she persisted, still straining to hold him away from her, though she knew her resolve was weakening.

His iron-muscled thigh ruthlessly forced between hers, holding them apart, making her devastatingly aware of the hardness of his male arousal, grinding against the very core of her body. 'Feel how much I want you,' he growled fiercely. 'Imagine what it would be like to feel me inside you—thrusting into you, till you're crying out with pleasure? Don't even try to deny that that's what you want—I can feel the way you're responding.'

She turned her head away, struggling for breath, struggling to resist the treacherous tug of desire that was dragging her down, making her long to surrender. 'No,' she persisted brokenly.

'Yes.'

The sheer power of his will was overcoming her determination, even though she knew that with one word of assent from her he would take her right here and now, and damn the risk that Barbara might come down and find them—the primeval forces driving him were that strong. She closed her eyes, torn by the conflict as her rational mind strained to form the word no, while a deeper impulse whispered, 'Yes...'

But before he could act on her helpless consent, there was a sound in the hall, and a familiar voice called, 'Lacey? Hi—I'm here! Any chance of a cuppa for a weary, footsore traveller?'

'*Hugo*?' She gasped in shock, dragging herself out of Jon's embrace and swiftly straightening her clothes.

'Damn!' muttered Jon impatiently. He caught her wrist as she ran towards the door, swinging her back against him. 'This is only a temporary reprieve,' he warned. 'Next time, I'll make damned sure we won't be disturbed.'

She stared at him, trembling inside, knowing that he had every intention of carrying out his threat. 'I'm not going to be your mistress,' she asserted, feeling no certainty whatsoever.

'Oh, yes, you are.' He laughed in arrogant contempt. 'It amuses me when you try to get on your high horse,' he taunted her, his eyes glittering. 'But don't think you fool me for a minute. You're a whore, available to any man who can afford to buy you. Well, from now on, I'm claiming exclusive use of your services—you'd better get used to that.'

She glared back at him defiantly, struggling to twist her wrist out of his grasp. 'Oh, yes? And what if I tell Barbara about it?' she challenged.

'Barbara understands these arrangements,' he responded, unruffled. 'It really wouldn't bother her at all.'

'Is that so? Well, bully for the pair of you. I always thought love came into marriage somewhere, but clearly I was wrong.'

'Merely naïve,' he grated, abruptly letting her go. 'We'd better go and say hello to your brother.'

CHAPTER SEVEN

'Hugo! What on earth are you doing here?' Lacey demanded, giving her twin a big hug. 'And how did you get into the house?'

He chuckled with laughter. 'I'm here to lend respectability to the situation,' he announced blithely. 'And that must be a first!'

'I contacted him last night,' Jon explained coolly, following her out into the hall.

Lacey stared from one to the other, frowning. '*You* contacted him? But . . . ?'

'You were concerned that the Press would make up stories about us,' he reminded her, his bland expression completely belying the fact that even the most scurrilous rag would have been hard pressed to invent anything steamier than what had just taken place in the parlour. 'But with your brother here, how could anyone possibly accuse us of running off to some cosy little love-nest? So I arranged to leave the back door key behind the water-butt, so that he could let himself in without the Press seeing him—that way we can make it appear as if he's been here all the time.'

'You *knew* he was my brother?' Lacey queried, startled.

'You let the pretence slip a couple of times, and I began to suspect,' he confirmed, an inflection of sardonic humour in his voice. 'I remembered that Clive had mentioned a brother, so I did a little checking.'

'Pretty neat strategy, I call it,' Hugo approved. 'Couldn't have thought of a better trick myself! Although,' he added, his eyes glinting with quizzical humour as he glanced from her to Jon, 'if I'm going to be in the way...?'

Lacey felt her cheeks flame scarlet, uncomfortable aware that her tousled hair and swollen lips probably betrayed all too clearly what he had interrupted with his arrival. 'Not at all,' she managed a little awkwardly. 'Actually that makes four of us—Jon's fiancée arrived a few hours ago.'

'Oh.' That single utterance conveyed that he had understood the position without the need for any further explanation. 'Well, that sounds like fun. What a pity I don't play bridge, or we could have had a good game.'

'We have Ludo,' Jon remarked with dry humour.

'Ah—that's more in my line...' His voice faded away, and Lacey glanced up at him in astonishment as she heard him whistle softly, his eyes lit up with frank appreciation as he gazed down the hall. She glanced back over her shoulder, and her heart sank; she might have known—Barbara was coming down the stairs. That sort of ice-cool blonde was exactly his type. As if there wasn't enough trouble already!

'Er...Barbara, this is my brother Hugo.' She hoped her swift warning frown would quell him. 'Hugo— this is Jon's fiancée.'

'Hi.' He met that haughty stare with one of his wickedest grins, and Lacey was a little surprised to see the other girl waver slightly.

'Good...afternoon,' she greeted him stiffly. But she quickly recovered, those diamond-chip eyes surveying the gathering with sardonic disdain. 'It seems to be getting a little crowded here,' she remarked mordantly. 'Are we expecting anyone else?'

'Not tonight,' Jon responded with a touch of dry humour; his shrewd eyes had missed nothing of the fleeting exchange between Hugo and his fiancée, but his reaction was impossible to read. 'Well, we don't want to stand around here in the hall all evening,' he added cordially. 'Why don't we go back upstairs?'

Barbara nodded a gracious assent, and turned to lead the way. Hugo's assessing gaze followed the sway of her slim *derrière* in the slightly clinging cashmere as she climbed the stairs, and Lacey glanced anxiously at Jon to see if he had noticed—but if he had, he had decided to do nothing at present.

She laid a detaining hand on her brother's arm. 'Don't,' she hissed.

He lifted his eyebrows in innocent question. 'Don't what?'

'She's Jon's fiancée,' she reminded him.

'I know.' But his wicked grin was unabashed, and there was a distinct air of arrogance in the set of his wide, well-muscled shoulders.

Lacey flashed him a severe look, but as Jon glanced back at them she quickly pinned a bright smile in place. 'Shall I put the kettle on?' she suggested. 'Tea, everyone?'

He lifted one dark eyebrow in sardonic amusement, mocking her for resorting to the time-honoured brew at every moment of awkwardness. But she refused to rise to the bait, making her escape to the kitchen, where Khan—who had been shut in there all afternoon—welcomed her with delight.

'Hello, baby.' She bent to ruffle his warm, soft fur. 'I know, it's rotten for you, stuck in here all by yourself—and I can't even take you out for a walk. I'll tell you what.' She hunkered down beside him as he nuzzled his cold nose against her ear. 'What about a biscuit? A nice choccy biscuit, eh?'

He slurped his pink tongue over her nose, and she laughed.

'You soppy thing. But at least all you want from me is a biscuit. Why can't all relationships be that simple?'

With a wistful sigh, she filled the kettle and got out the teacups. Nothing that involved Jon Parrish could ever be simple—he was a very clever, very devious man. She had to admire the strategy he had concocted to outwit the Press—though it scared her a little too. How could she ever hope to escape the coils of such a skilled manipulator?

She would really have preferred not to have to think about what had happened in the parlour just before Hugo had arrived, but the memory of that fierce, demanding kiss still seemed to be imprinted on her mouth. Why had she let it happen? She could certainly be under no illusion—he had made it more than clear what he thought of her. He still believed she had been his stepfather's mistress, and seemed to take it for granted that she would now be willing to be his— even after his marriage.

She paused for a moment in what she was doing, and just stood staring blankly at the wall. His mistress... The images the word conjured up swirled in her brain; of gleaming naked bodies, and long, sizzling nights of wicked sex... After all, she could never aspire to be his wife, even if Barbara wasn't on the scene. By being his mistress, at least she would have some part of him...

Shocked at the train of her own thoughts, she shook her head. She dared not let herself be lured down that path. Quite apart from the fact that it was entirely against everything she believed in to have an affair with a married man, she knew she wouldn't be able to keep it purely physical, as he intended. She would be in serious danger of falling in love with him.

Resolutely ignoring the sharp twist of pain in her heart, she picked up the tray and carried it carefully upstairs.

They were in the largest bedroom, at the front of the house—the one Jon had slept in last night. It had a big, old-fashioned double bed, and Lacey had been trying all afternoon not to let herself think about him sharing it with Barbara tonight.

Barbara was sitting in the armchair, and Hugo had turned a straight-back chair around and was perched across it, leaning on its back in a pose of casual energy, engaging her in flirtatious conversation. He had tossed his ancient leather jacket on the bed, and his sleeveless T-shirt showed off his magnificently muscled body to perfection—and although she was still trying to maintain her cool façade, it was evident that she was far from immune to his implied flattery, nor to his striking physical attraction.

Lacey slanted a covert glance towards Jon. He was leaning against the mantelshelf, apparently quite unconcerned about what was going on between the other two. Although perhaps that was only to be expected, she acknowledged thoughtfully—partisan as she was regarding her handsome brother, she knew he was no match for Jonathan Parrish.

She had to admit that she was a little surprised that Barbara had shown even a flicker of interest—she wouldn't have thought a muscle-bound hulk several years her junior would have appealed to one of her refined and sophisticated tastes.

Or maybe she was just using Hugo to indulge in a little subtle revenge for Jon's behaviour? That was understandable—he certainly deserved it. So long as Hugo didn't get hurt—beneath that tough act he put on Lacey knew there was a soft heart, and she was quite sure that Barbara wouldn't spare a thought for his feelings.

Setting down the tea tray, she handed out the cups. Then she sat down on the end of the bed, firmly engaging her brother's attention. 'So, how did you get up here?' she asked. 'Surely you didn't hitch-hike all the way?'

He shook his hand. 'I got a train to Newcastle, and then hitched the rest of the way,' he responded, reaching out for one of the chocolate biscuits she had brought up with the tea. 'I managed to pick up a lorry on Mosley Street almost straight away, and he brought me all the way up to the turn-off for Elsdon. After that a farmer gave me a lift. I had to walk the last five miles, though,' he added with feeling.

'Oh, poor thing,' she teased affectionately. 'It's good exercise.'

He laughed—he knew that his easy sense of humour was one of his most attractive characteristics—and slid an appealing glance towards Barbara. 'I knew I'd get no sympathy from her,' he protested. 'She's quite heartless.'

Barbara was forced into a reluctant smile. 'I'm not sure that I sympathise with you either,' she responded carefully. 'Five miles isn't very far.'

'Ah, cruel,' he accused, his eyes dancing.

Lacey flicked another covert glance up at Jon. He was sipping his tea, quietly watching the exchange between the other two, his expression completely unreadable. What was he thinking? It made her a little nervous to wonder if he was concealing anger at Hugo's behaviour; he had already proved that he could be a very dangerous enemy.

This was getting ridiculous, she reflected a little wildly—there was Jon, playing the irreproachably respectable fiancé but relentlessly pursuing her in secret, while his fiancée appeared to be succumbing to the blandishments of her brother! It had to be a pretty strange kind of engagement.

But there could be no doubt that it was genuine; Barbara was wearing a ring on the third finger of her left hand—a very large ring, consisting of a square-cut emerald surrounded by diamonds. Maybe Jon was right—maybe she *was* naïve. Clearly in his world, at least, such things were very different from what they were in hers—after all, his own parents' marriage seemed to have little to do with love, and everything to do with outward respectability and social standing.

But she had no intention of letting herself get involved in such an arrangement, she vowed resolutely. In her book, love and marriage went hand in hand—and she didn't want to compromise on that. Not even for Jon Parrish.

At last a glance at her watch told her that it was time to start preparing dinner. She rose to her feet and began to collect up the teacups. 'There's not a lot of stuff left in the pantry, but I could do a vegetarian curry,' she offered diffidently.

'Great!' Hugo approved with relish. 'My favourite. Do you like curry, Babs?'

Her eyes flicked with a half-hearted indignation at his familiarity in shortening her name, but she couldn't suppress a reluctant smile. 'Certainly,' she conceded. 'There's a very good restaurant off Kensington Church Street—do you know it?'

'Not really my side of town,' he responded with a provocative grin. 'But I'll tell you what—there's a great tandoori down the Old Kent Road. I'll take you there one of these days.'

To Lacey's amazement, the normally so self-possessed blonde actually blushed! Her brother seemed to be succeeding in melting that ice-cool exterior. But she wished he wouldn't; it was only going to add to the complications. She flickered a swift glance in Jon's direction to see how he had reacted to that blatant incursion, but it was impossible to read that enigmatic expression.

She was a little reluctant to go down to the kitchen and leave them, worrying what might happen. But if they were going to eat, she would have to. And after all, Hugo was a grown man, she reminded herself firmly—he was exactly the same age as she was, though sometimes it was easy to forget it. If he got himself into a sticky situation, he would just have to get himself out!

Khan was delighted to see her, and more than wiling to help with the dinner by clearing up the peelings of all the vegetables. She laughed at him as he dived into them as if they were a gourmet feast. 'You'd eat any-thing!' she chided. 'It's a wonder you're not as fat as a barrel!'

'Afghans don't get fat,' Jon commented, strolling into the kitchen. 'Yes, all right, boy—I can tell you're delighted to see me.' He caught the dog's front paws as he excitedly tried to lick his face. 'That's enough—down, now.'

Khan instantly recognised that masterful tone, and plopped his backside on the floor, his front paws beautifully together, his tail wildly sweeping the uneven quarry tiles.

Lacey laughed. 'Why does he always do as you say? He never obeys me as quickly as that.'

'You're too soft with him,' Jon advised her with a hint of mocking humour. 'He knows he can wind you round his paw whenever he wants to.'

'I suppose so,' she conceded wryly. 'I just can't help thinking about how nearly he was put down—he's such a loving dog.' She glanced up at Jon, wondering why he had come downstairs—deliberately leaving Barbara and Hugo alone in the bedroom. It was almost as if he *wanted* them to start something.

He came across to the table, slanting a faintly sar-donic look at the pile of cleaned and chopped veg-etables. 'You've been working hard again,' he remarked. 'You don't have to, you know. We could have made do with sandwiches or something.'

She shrugged her slender shoulders, half turning away from him to continue slicing the carrots. 'Oh,

I enjoy cooking,' she demurred. 'Besides, vegetable curry isn't hard to make.'

He had come up close behind her, and slid his arms around her waist, drawing her back forcefully against him. 'You've been dusting and polishing and doing the housework all day,' he grated, a sharp edge of impatience in his voice. 'As if you were some kind of servant.'

'Well, isn't that how you see me?' she demanded tautly, struggling to fight the treacherous weakness that was flooding through her. 'To serve your sexual demands, if not your domestic ones?'

'If that's how you choose to interpret it.' His breath was hot against the nape of her neck, stirring her hair, and his hands had slipped up to mould her ripe, round breasts, caressing them with ruthless sensuality. 'But don't try to pretend it's only my needs we're talking about here. I can feel your needs every time I touch you.'

'You . . . shouldn't even be touching me at all,' she protested raggedly, unable to push him away. 'Your fiancée is upstairs . . .'

'Talking to your brother. I thought I'd leave them alone to get . . . better acquainted.'

'Don't you realise what's going on?' Her breathing was shallow and agitated, each breath crushing her aching breasts invitingly into his palms. 'He's not just talking to her—he's trying to chat her up.'

'I know,' he conceded, chuckling wickedly. 'That's proved to be quite an unexpected bonus. He's keeping her occupied . . .'

'While you're down here with me!' she concluded, appalled at such blatant cynicism.

'Exactly.' With an almost imperceptible hardening of his muscles he prevented her from escaping him, holding her against him as his hot tongue explored the delicate shell of her ear.

'What if she decides that's what's sauce for the goose is sauce for the gander?' she demanded, trying in vain not to let herself respond to what he was doing to her. 'Wouldn't you even care about that?'

'On the contrary—I think I'd find it quite amusing,' he countered. 'Wouldn't you?'

'No! Maybe that's the way couples behave in your world, but they don't in mine—and I don't like it, I won't be part of it.'

'But you can't escape, can you?' he taunted softly. 'It's your destiny. You were created solely for the purpose of giving a man satisfaction—and that man is going to be me.'

With deliberate intent he slid his hands up beneath her sweater, and eased the tight lace cups of her bra up over the swelling curves of her breasts. She drew in a sharp breath as she felt his touch, cool and tantalising against her heated skin, but she couldn't stop him—she was a helpless co-conspirator, colluding in her own downfall. Her head fell back against his shoulder, and she heard herself moaning softly; her bones were melting to jelly, and if he weren't holding her up she would have slid to the floor.

'This is the only thing I've been able to think about since the first time I met you,' he growled huskily. 'These beautiful, ripe, round breasts—so firm and abundant. I've dreamed of how they would look when you were naked, how they would feel to my touch, how they would taste . . . how I would caress them . . .'

His clever fingers were toying with her tender nipples, pinching at them in sweet torment. 'And now that I know, the temptation to enjoy them is only getting stronger. I don't think I could ever get enough of them.'

'Is... that all you want from me?' she demanded on a sobbing breath.

He laughed in biting mockery, deliberately mis-understanding her words. 'You know it isn't. I want all of you. I want the smooth, sweet silk of your skin, the peachy curve of your stomach, the downy blonde curls between your thighs...' He bent his head to sink his teeth erotically into the curve of her shoulder, his body crushed so intimately close against hers that she could feel the pressure of his hard male arousal. 'I want to lay you down on your back, and feel you moving beneath me, feel your thighs yielding to mine, feel the moist, warm core of your body surrender as I take you...'

With a strangled choke of panic she jerked herself out of his grasp, and retreated to the far side of the table, the chopping knife still in her hand.

His hard mouth had curved into a sardonic smile. 'You look as if you're planning to use that knife on me.'

'I just might do that if you touch me again!' she threatened, her eyes spitting fire.

He chuckled softly. 'In that case, perhaps I'd better take Khan out for a walk after all.'

She blinked at him in blank surprise, caught off balance by his unexpected change of direction. 'But... what about the reporters?' she queried, be-wildered. 'Won't they pester you?'

'They're all at the front at the moment—it looks as if one of them's just got back from the chip-shop with their dinner. I'm surprised you didn't offer them some curry,' he added, his eyes glinting with teasing amusement. 'If I slip out across the yard and over the fields they won't see me. Besides, my ankle's feeling better now, and I could do with a bit of exercise.' He took the lead down from its hook on the back of the door, and Khan went wild, chasing round and round the kitchen, barking excitedly. 'I think that settles it,' he remarked with a grin. 'Come on then, you daft mutt, stand still for a moment while I get your lead on.'

Lacey was forced to smile. 'Thank you. I was getting a bit worried about him, not being able to go out—he does love to have a walk. Don't let him off the lead, though—I don't want to risk him running off and worrying sheep.'

'OK. Lock the door behind me. I'll be about half an hour.'

She nodded. 'Dinner'll be ready by then.'

'Good.' As he walked to the door, he paused very close to her, and she found herself captured by that dark, hypnotic gaze. 'By the way, I shouldn't rely on that knife to defend yourself,' he warned softly. 'I could take it off you in a second.'

She gasped as he did just that, slipping it out of her hand and laying it down on the table with a taunting smile. She stared up at him, her heartbeat racing. It was true—he could disarm all her defences just as easily. She was finding it harder and harder to resist the aching longing that was growing inside her—it frightened her to realise how easy it would be to succumb.

He laughed, low and husky, and leaning towards her brushed his mouth lightly over hers. 'Take that on account,' he murmured. 'Until later.'

He let himself out of the back door, and she closed it quickly behind him, turning the big old-fashioned key in the lock. It took her several moments to steady her ragged breathing. Things were getting dangerously out of control, and she didn't know what to do about it.

But she had no intention of letting him use her for sex—because that was what it would amount to, she acknowledged painfully. It was humiliating to think that that was still how he saw her—but then she had done little to convince him that she wasn't that 'type'. She had been far too willing to succumb to temptation each time he had kissed her, responding to his caresses with a wantonness that would have given him every reason to suppose that ultimately she could be persuaded to become his mistress, in spite of her protestations.

And, to her shame, she *had* been half-ready to consider it. Lord, where was her self-respect? Well, from now on she was going to have to make it very clear that she was not interested in the kind of relationship he had in mind. It wasn't going to be easy, but the first place to start was inside her own head. No more indulgence in dangerous fantasies; Jon Parrish was as strictly off-limits as chocolate when she was on a diet.

'...Six, seven, eight, *nine*! That's another of your counters knocked out.' Hugo slanted Barbara a look of devilish wickedness as he pounced on the Ludo board. 'You're losing to me hands down.'

Barbara shrugged her elegant shoulders in a gesture of mild disdain for the childish game—though to Lacey's amused astonishment she had been entering into it with as much spirit as the rest of them.

They had set the board out after dinner, and already they had played three games by the flickering light of half a dozen candles. It was really quite cosy in the parlour; they had put the board on a low table, drawing three armchairs close around it—Hugo was sitting on the floor. To begin with, he had been resting against Lacey's chair, but somehow he had subtly shifted, so that now he was resting against Barbara's.

'Anyway, I already have two counters home, and you only have one,' Barbara pointed out coolly, shaking the dice in her hand; the interest with which she leaned forward to count up her score betrayed her reluctant enjoyment of this unsophisticated pastime. 'Seven. Hah! I've got you this time—serves you right!'

Lacey glanced up from beneath her lashes at Jon as he took the dice. His manner all evening had been the same—casual and relaxed, giving no sign that he minded in the least that Hugo was flirting quite outrageously with his fiancée.

Well, it was no concern of hers, she reminded herself crisply. She had already vowed that she wouldn't get drawn into it. Except that she couldn't help thinking about tonight. There were only two bedrooms prepared—the small one she had slept in, and the master bedroom where Jon had slept, with its wide double bed. No one had said anything about needing to prepare any others, so she hadn't done anything about it either.

But she didn't want to think about the implications—that Barbara would be sharing Jon's bed. Of course she would—they were engaged to be married, they must sleep together regularly. Suddenly she felt her mouth go dry, and the heat of the fire seemed almost unbearable...

'It's your turn.'

Jon was holding out the dice to her, the mocking glint in his dark eyes warning her that he could guess what kind of thoughts were running through her mind. Steeling her nerves, she returned him a look of cool indifference, and took the dice from him.

'What do I need?' she enquired lightly, glancing at the board. 'A five—to win!' She blew on the dice for luck, and tossed them on to the board. They came up four and one, and with a crow of triumph she counted her last piece home.

'Well done!' Hugo teased her. 'Now we've won one each.' He yawned, stretching his arms above his head. 'Another game, anyone?'

'No, I...think I'll call it a night now,' Lacey demurred. 'I'll just do the washing up before I go to bed——'

'Leave that—Hugo and I will do it,' Jon cut in briskly, sweeping the pieces from the board and stowing them on the mantelpiece. 'You don't have to wait on us hand and foot.'

She couldn't mistake that deliberate invocation of their earlier conversation in the kitchen, but chose to ignore it. The two men collected up the teacups and took them out to the kitchen, leaving the women alone

together; as soon as they were gone, Lacey sensed the
knives being sharpened.

'So—you're an actress,' Barbara cooed in saccharine tones. 'Have you ever been in anything I
would have seen?'

'I doubt it.' Lacey deliberately kept her reply am-
biguous. 'But then it depends on what sort of thing
you watch.'

'Yes, I . . . suppose it does.' Barbara's disdainful expression betrayed that her imagination was running
away with her. 'And . . . your brother—what does he
do?'

Lacey smiled slowly to herself—she was going to
love this! 'He's a male stripper,' she replied blandly.

The other girl almost choked. 'You're not serious!'

'Of course! He dances with a group called *Les
Sauvages*—you may have heard of them?'

'No, I . . . can't say that I have . . .'

'They're making quite a name for themselves,'
Lacey added informatively. 'They're really very good.
You should go and watch them some time—I'm sure
he'd get you a ticket.'

Barbara seemed to be having trouble speaking.
'I'm . . . not sure that it's really my kind of thing.'

'No?' purred Lacey sweetly. 'Pity. Well, I think I'll
go up to bed now—goodnight.'

She breezed from the room, her spirits buoyed up
by that little confrontation. But as she started to climb
the stairs, Jon came out into the hall.

'Rushing away?' he taunted softly.

'I'm tired,' she responded, her eyes cool.

He leaned on the carved newel-post at the foot of
the stairs, a sardonic smile curving that intriguing

mouth. 'I wondered if you'd thought about the sleeping arrangements for tonight?' he queried. 'There are only two bedrooms ready.'

'I know,' she responded. 'Hugo can sleep in the parlour—it's the warmest room in the house besides the kitchen, and he'll be quite comfortable in an armchair for tonight.'

'Ah ... of course.'

He said nothing more, merely smiling in that infuriatingly enigmatic way, and Lacey continued on her way up to bed. But that fleeting glow of triumph over her rival was soon extinguished; she hadn't needed him to rub it in about the bed situation—she had already come to terms with it.

But even so, it was far from easy to undress and slip between the sheets in her own small room, knowing that on the other side of the stairs he and Barbara would be together, sharing the warmth of each other's bodies, holding each other and making love far into the night.

In vain she hugged the pillow. Her whole body ached with the need to feel his kisses and caresses, to yield to the hard thrust of his possession; and knowing that he was so close, but with someone else, made it a hundred times worse.

Khan, sleeping across her feet as usual, seemed to sense her pain, and crept up the bed to nuzzle against her. 'Oh, Khan,' she sighed, burrowing her face into his soft fur for comfort, 'what an idiot I am. I've gone and fallen in love with the rat—but all he wants from me is sex. What am I going to do?'

Those liquid brown eyes sympathised earnestly as he licked the tears from her cheeks with his big pink tongue.

She laughed, and cuddled him close. 'At least you'll always love me, won't you?' she murmured. 'And I'll always love you. No matter what happens, it'll always be you and me.' And with one arm curled around his warm body, she finally managed to drift off to sleep.

'I just wish you'd stop it, that's all,' Lacey insisted forcefully, taking out her frustration on the dirty breakfast plates she was washing up. 'She's his fiancée, for goodness' sake!'

Hugo grinned mischievously. 'So you keep saying.'

'What do you mean, so I keep saying? Haven't you noticed that dirty great big emerald ring she's wearing on the third finger of her left hand? What do you think that is? Scotch mist?'

'Well,' he taunted, his expression bland, 'either they're a very old-fashioned couple—which I can't see, somehow—or else there's rather less to it than meets the eye.'

She stared up at him, puzzled. 'What do you mean?'

'They didn't sleep together last night,' he informed her smugly.

Her heart kicked against her chest, and she had to struggle to keep her voice steady. 'But... There were only two beds aired ready,' she frowned. 'The one I slept in, and the one in Jon's room.'

'Yes. And Babs slept in the one in Jon's room, while he stayed downstairs in the other armchair in the front room—all night!'

'Well... But that doesn't mean a thing,' she argued a little uncertainly. 'Maybe they were both just too tired. Or... or maybe they *are* waiting until they get married.'

'Well, I'm sure you know Jon better than I do,' he persisted. 'Do *you* think he's the kind to wait two years?'

'I...I don't know. I mean...it's not as if... People like that don't marry for the same reasons as we do. It's got more to do with wealth and social standing. I mean, look at his own parents—his mother tolerates his stepfather's affairs so as not to upset the apple-cart with his career.'

Hugo shook his hand, unconvinced. 'That's as maybe. But if you ask me, she won't be wearing that ring much longer.'

Lacey shook her head, refusing to let herself be carried away by such dangerous optimism. 'I don't think you're right,' she insisted. 'I mean, just because she seems to be letting you chat her up... She isn't going to let it go any further.'

'Want to bet?' he challenged. 'Five quid on it?'

She slanted him an anxious look. 'Hugo, you're not really...*serious* about her, are you?'

He chuckled with pure lascivious wickedness. 'Don't worry,' he assured her. 'I'm not planning to fall in love with her. I just fancy the idea of being a toy-boy for a while.'

'Hugo!' She stared at him in shock. 'How could you?'

'Why not?' he argued innocently. 'There's no harm in it—we're both old enough to know what we're doing. Besides, while I'm keeping her entertained it leaves you a free hand with lover-boy, doesn't it?'

'He's not my lover-boy!' she protested, her cheeks flushing a vivid shade of scarlet.

'No?' His smile was affectionately teasing. 'He was asking an awful lot of questions about you last night.'

'Was he?' She looked up at him quickly, and then looked away again, forcibly suppressing the hope that had sprung to her eyes. 'What did you tell him?'

'That you're a sweet old-fashioned girl, and if anyone messes with you I'll knock their teeth down their throat,' he responded grimly.

'You didn't!' She laughed, trying for a lightness of tone. 'I don't suppose he believed you, anyway.'

'He should have—I meant it,' Hugo asserted, an irrepressible twinkle in his eyes. 'Not that I'm sure I could do it, mind. Anyway, we'll see who's right, won't we?' he added with a cheerful shrug. 'It could get quite interesting.'

Lacey slanted him a worried glance. He had all the arrogant self-assurance of youth, but she was afraid that this time he could fall flat on his face. Barbara wasn't one of his usual dilly-headed young things— she was a mature and sophisticated woman, with a successful career and a mind of her own.

But at that moment, Barbara herself came into the kitchen, and it would have been absolutely impossible to misinterpret the coy look she slanted at him, nor the coquettishness of her smile.

'Ah, there you are, Hugo,' she purred. 'I was looking for you. I need to move my bed—I'm sure that wall is damp. Do you think you could come and help me?'

'Of course.' He grinned lazily, leaning down close to Lacey's ear as he folded the tea towel he had been using to help with the drying up. 'Five quid,' he reminded her softly.

Lacey clenched her jaw, scrubbing viciously at a burnt-on scrap of scrambled egg. This whole thing was getting so crazy she had given up trying to be rational about it. Maybe she *was* old-fashioned; why should she be shocked at the idea of Hugo's being Barbara's toy-boy? After all, as he had said, they were both old enough to know what they were doing.

And it was no worse than what she had been doing with Jon. Maybe she should agree to become his mistress—why not? Everyone else seemed to regard it as a perfectly normal thing to do, to be engaged to one person while indulging every vice imaginable with someone else. Everyone but naïve, innocent Lacey, who was still foolish enough to want to believe in love.

CHAPTER EIGHT

'MORE housework?'

Lacy started as Jon walked into the kitchen, although she had been on tenterhooks all morning, anticipating that he would come down. Her elbow knocked sharply against the door of the cupboard she was tidying out, and she uttered a sharp cry of pain.

'Careful,' he teased, helping her to her feet. 'Are you all right?'

'Yes, thank you.' She moved away from him, rubbing her elbow, struggling to maintain a semblance of composure even though her heartbeat was accelerating out of control. 'Er... Would you like...?'

'A cup of tea?' he guessed, that firm mouth curving into the smile she found so disturbingly attractive. 'That seems like a good idea.'

As she pottered around putting the kettle on, Lacey could feel him watching her, those dark eyes strangely unreadable; it gave her an odd, trembly feeling inside, as if her bones were slowly melting to jelly. Ever since Hugo had first told her of it, she had been trying hard not to let herself read too much significance into the fact that Jon hadn't spent the night with Barbara. After all, there could be any number of perfectly good reasons for it ... It was just that none of the ones that seemed logical made any sense, and none of the ones that made sense seemed logical.

She poured the tea, and took it over to the table, sitting down opposite him. 'It's keeping nice and warm in here, isn't it?' she remarked, trying for a conversational tone. 'That range is really good. Do we have enough wood to keep it going?'

'There's plenty,' he assured her, the faint flicker of amusement in his eyes telling her that he was well aware that she was talking just to cover her nervousness. 'I had a look in the loft, and there's an old chest of drawers in there that will cut up, and some more chairs. We've enough to withstand a siege.'

She managed a rather forced laugh, slanting her eyes towards the window. 'I hope we won't have to,' she sighed. 'Surely they'll get fed up soon, and go away?'

'I wouldn't count on it,' he advised drily. 'I think we've probably got a few more days of this, at the least.'

'Oh, well.' She shrugged her slender shoulders in a dismissive gesture, although her heart was pattering much too rapidly at the thought of being trapped here with him for several more days. But then of course, Barbara would be here too, she reminded herself—and Hugo. He surely wouldn't try to force the issue while they were living right under their noses—would he?

'You seem to have accepted the prospect philosophically at last,' he commented, regarding her across the table with that level gaze she always found so disconcerting.

She conceded a slightly crooked smile. 'There doesn't seem to be very much I can do about it.'

'Why didn't you tell me that the play you were talking about was one you're producing with mentally handicapped kids?' he asked bluntly.

She felt a flush of pink rise to her cheeks; damn Hugo! 'They're not called mentally handicapped these days,' she responded, sidestepping the main issue. 'It's society that handicaps them. Most of them are perfectly capable—they just need a little more time than other people to learn things, so we say they have a developmental impairment.'

'Fair enough,' he responded, his dark eyes glinting with mild amusement at her evasion. 'Why did you let me think it was that awful farce thing you were in that was so important to you?'

'I never said a thing,' she retorted. 'You just jumped to that conclusion.'

'So I did. I jumped to a lot of conclusions. But you didn't do a great deal to disabuse me of them.'

'I tried,' she reminded him indignantly. 'But you were so damned convinced I was having an affair with your stepfather, nothing I could have said would have made the least difference. What did you want? An affidavit signed in blood?'

A faint smile curved the corners of his hard mouth. 'It might have helped if you hadn't been swanning around in that rather fetching pink thing,' he remarked. 'It wasn't exactly conducive to clear thinking.'

'I wasn't wearing it when you came up to our flat,' she pointed out with a touch of asperity. 'It didn't seem to make any difference.'

'True,' he acknowledged wryly. 'But by then it wasn't so much what you were wearing as my vivid recollection of what was underneath it that was causing the problem.' His gaze slid down, lingering over the firm, round contours of her body, and he seemed to have difficulty dragging it back to her face. 'And you have to admit, though you might have been protesting your innocence, your behaviour didn't exactly serve to convince.'

'I didn't...' The pink in her cheeks flamed to a deeper scarlet. 'It wasn't...'

'My conversation with your brother was quite illuminating in a number of respects,' he remarked, those dark eyes glinting with a faintly mocking amusement. 'Though I'm not quite sure if I believe what he said one hundred per cent; oh, I'm sure he thought he was telling the truth—it just seems a little...far-fetched.'

She knew exactly what he was talking about, and tilted up her chin in a show of defiance, though she couldn't quite meet his eyes. 'Why should it be farfetched?' she enquired tautly.

He laughed, a low, husky chuckle. 'You know why. It would be very flattering to think I'm the first man who's been able to arouse you like that, but even I'm not that conceited.'

'You surprise me,' she retorted, throwing him an acid glance. 'I'd have thought you'd be well able to believe it.'

A flicker of sharp interest glinted in his eyes. '*Is* it true?' he asked.

She would have preferred not to answer, but that hypnotic gaze seemed to have subordinated her will. 'Yes,' she conceded with a snap. 'It is.'

He leaned back in his seat, slowly sipping his tea. 'Well, well,' he mused. 'So you never did have an affair with my stepfather?'

'No. Nor with Ted, nor with anyone else. And I've never tried to blackmail anyone either.'

'I'd already worked that one out,' he responded with a smile. 'If anyone had being trying to blackmail Clive, he'd have come straight to me. It was rather foolish of him to lie to the Press, of course, but then grace under pressure never was his strong point. I suspect that having seen that rather dazzling photograph of you, he was afraid that no one would believe his relationship with you could possibly be innocent, so he decided to portray himself as the injured party.'

She stared at him, her heartbeat fluttering like butterflies' wings. 'You . . . really believe me now?' she whispered.

'Yes.' He leaned across the table and took her small hand gently in his, his thumb brushing lightly over the pale skin inside her wrist where her pulses raced in agitation. 'I'm sorry I didn't believe you in the first place,' he murmured softly. 'It was all such a very familiar story—the beautiful young blonde, his indignant denials. There seemed no reason to suppose that this was any different from all the other times— I'm afraid I was so convinced of your guilt before I'd even met you that even if you'd looked like a Sunday school teacher I wouldn't have been able to change my mind. And you don't look like a Sunday school teacher,' he added with a crooked smile.

She forced herself to return him a level look. 'Am I suppose to take that as a compliment?' she enquired coolly.

A dark flame flickered briefly in his eyes. 'Of course.'

She felt the heat coursing through her blood, as if she had a fever, and struggled to find a way to turn the conversation back. 'Did Clive have . . . a lot of affairs, then?' she managed.

'Dozens.' There was an unmistakable trace of bitterness in his voice. 'Even before he married my mother I caught him coming out of the linen cupboard with one of the maids, wiping her lipstick off his mouth. Of course I couldn't say anything—I was only seven, I didn't even really understand what was going on. And I was packed off to boarding school a little while after that.'

'Didn't your mother know what he was like?'

'Yes, she did. But she didn't really care. You see, she'd loved my father very much—she'd married him in spite of all her family's objections. After he died, she returned home, and I don't think she ever had any intention of marrying again. Then Clive came along, and my grandfather wanted her to marry him— the family have been active in politics for generations, and there was no one to carry on the direct line. He wanted a son-in-law who would keep up the tradition, and Clive saw it as a way of ensuring his selection for a nice safe seat.'

'So they *forced* her to marry him?' Lacey queried, appalled.

He shook his head. 'Oh, it wasn't as melodramatic as that. She wanted to get away from her parents, have a home of her own again. She's very fond of gardening, and so long as she had a couple of acres to potter about in, she was quite happy. And Clive always had to be very discreet about his activities, so she wasn't bothered. It was an arrangement that suited her very well.'

'I see.' And a little boy had been sent away from home just when he was at his most confused and vulnerable. And what an example he had had to grow up with! No wonder he was so cynical about marriage, separating his expectations of a wife so neatly from his physical needs—and leaving no place for love. How different it all was from her own childhood; money had been tight, but there had be no shortage of love in their plain little south London council flat.

'Did Hugo tell you I'd offered him a job?' Jon enquired, switching the subject.

'No?' She glanced across at him in surprise. 'Doing what?'

'The leisure development team. They look at projects to use the land that's being taken out of agricultural production—golf courses, nature parks and the like. I thought he might find it interesting.'

'Yes!' she agreed readily. 'It would be right up his street. Thank you.'

'He turned it down.'

Her eyes clouded with disappointment. 'Oh, no! Of all the stupid...! Oh, listen, just let me have a word with him—I'm sure I'll be able to persuade him to change his mind.'

He smiled with a trace of irony. 'I don't think you need worry about your brother,' he remarked. 'He's got his head well screwed on when it comes to future plans. He told me what he's got in mind, and I think it will work out very well.'

Lacey stared at him blankly. 'You mean he's really serious about starting up his own business?'

'Of course he is.'

She laughed, mildly bemused. 'I thought he was just fobbing me off. I suppose I still tend to think of him as a rowdy teenager—I tend to forget we're the same age.'

'Girls often grow up quicker than boys,' he concurred. 'But he's making up ground fast. You don't need to mother him any more.'

'I don't!' she protested.

'Don't you?' Those dark, perceptive eyes challenged her.

'Well, maybe a bit,' she conceded with a reluctant smile. 'Even when Mum was alive—she worked long hours, you see, and shifts, so quite often she wasn't home in the evenings and we had to fend for ourselves. She used to worry that Hughie would go off the rails with some of the gangs that used to hang about round the streets, so I used to try and keep an eye on him a bit.'

'I think she'd be very proud of him if she could see him now,' he remarked softly. 'And of you.'

The hot colour rushed back into her cheeks. 'Oh, no, I . . . I'm not very good at anything. I'm not even much of an actress—I just enjoy it. I don't think I'm ever going to be rich and famous.'

'You have a kind heart,' he countered. 'That's worth far more than any amount of success.'

She lowered her eyes, struggling to control her ragged breathing. *He's engaged to Barbara*, she was forced to remind herself. Besides, it wasn't exactly a lover-like statement. She must have imagined the way he seemed to be looking at her. Wanting a thing didn't make it so.

'I . . . I'd better go and finish dusting the sitting-room,' she muttered awkwardly. 'It's . . . best to keep on top of it.'

He didn't try to prevent her escape, and some time later she heard him go upstairs.

Lacey lay in bed, gazing at the dying embers of the fire that were still glowing in the grate, giving out just enough heat to keep the November chill from the room. It was half an hour past midnight, but she was a long way from sleep.

Since that conversation in the kitchen she hadn't been alone with Jon again, but she had been uneasily aware of him every moment of the time. She had tried hard to conceal the way she was feeling, afraid that Barbara might notice something amiss—although Barbara had seemed so interested in Hugo that Lacey wondered if she would have noticed if she and Jon had started making love on the floor right in front of her!

Not that it made any difference, she reflected wistfully. Even if it hadn't been for Barbara, the position would have been exactly the same. Not that she could complain that he hadn't been honest with her—he had made it clear from the beginning that he only wanted her body. He hadn't asked her to fall in love with him.

And where was he sleeping tonight? Downstairs in the parlour again—or with his fiancée? She didn't care to think about that one too closely. Slipping out of bed, she peeped through the curtains to look down into the yard. The pressmen had retreated to their cars; it must be very cold and uncomfortable trying to sleep like that, but she was finding it hard to feel still any sympathy for them. If only they would give up and go away, and leave her in peace! If it weren't for them, she could go away from here, forget she had ever met Jon Parrish.

Only it wouldn't be that easy, she acknowledged wryly. Somehow, in spite of all her intentions to the contrary, she had fallen in love with him, and nothing was ever going to make that go away.

In spite of the fire it was quite cold, and she reached for the old raincoat she had worn to wrap on over her skimpy nightdress. She wasn't going to be able to sleep, so she might as well go downstairs and make herself a cup of tea. Khan, snoozing comfortably at the foot of her bed, lifted one enquiring eyebrow and decided to go with her, pausing first to have a long, lazy stretch and then to scratch a wayward flea.

The kitchen was warm and cosy. She lit a couple of candles, and filled the kettle, and sat down in the shabby armchair beside the range to wait for it to boil. Khan went snuffling off around the corners of the room, ever hopeful of finding a forgotten crumb of food, or a spider to play with.

She was almost dozing when a sudden cold draught struck her shoulder, and she glanced round to find that he had pushed open the door to the passage between the pantry and the scullery. Quickly she jumped up, and ran to find out what he was up to.

The passage led towards the derelict stable-block; there was a door, strongly bolted into its frame, but the panels were rotting away, and Khan had clearly been helping them, to judge from the fresh teeth-marks in the wood. She would have to find something to nail over the gap tomorrow, or he would soon be able to get out.

'No!' she scolded him sharply. 'Bad boy.'

Those liquid brown eyes gazed up at her in abject apology, and he rubbed himself against her legs, stretching up his fine head to implore her to love him. She laughed, ruffling his yellow fringe.

'You rascal—you mustn't go running off around here. If a farmer caught you worrying his sheep he could shoot you.' She looked around, and found an odd piece of wood to cover the hole in the door, propping it in place with a chair. Khan watched her with alert curiosity, wagging his tail. 'There—that'll do till the morning,' she told him. 'Come on, let's go and see if that kettle's boiled.'

He skipped ahead of her into the kitchen, yapping with delight, and as she followed she realised why; Jon was there. He had shaved this morning, bor-rowing Hugo's razor, but already that hint of shadow was darkening his jaw with its gypsy raffishness. He was still wearing the shirt he had had on during the day, but the buttons weren't fastened—and though the muscles across his lightly bronzed chest were not quite so magnificently developed as her brother's, that tall, wide-shouldered frame was clearly in excellent condition.

He glanced up as she came in, a faintly sardonic smile curving that disturbingly sensual mouth. 'Having trouble sleeping?'

'I...just thought I'd have a cup of tea,' she choked out, the rapid acceleration of her heartbeat making her feel a little dizzy.

He came towards her, those dark eyes glinting with lazy mockery. 'At every crisis point of your life, you always run to make a pot of tea,' he teased gently.

'I don't,' she protested, her voice peaking with agitation. 'I just... It doesn't have to be a crisis.'

'Why couldn't you sleep?' he taunted, his eyes challenging her to tell the truth.

'I...I...'

'Oh, Lacey...' He reached out and caught her wrist, drawing her inexorably into his arms. 'What are we going to do about this?'

A ragged sob broke from her lips, and she buried her face against the solid wall of his chest. 'I...I don't know,' she whispered.

'Don't you?' He put his hand beneath her chin, tilting up her face to his. Those dark fires had ignited in his eyes, flaming with a heat that scorched her soul. 'I do.'

His mouth came down on hers, hot and demanding; and though the guilt of knowing that what she was doing was wrong tore at her heart, she could only surrender. His lips were moving over hers, coaxing and inciting them to part and permit him to plunder deep into the sweetest depths of her mouth, his languorous tongue swirling over the delicate inner membranes, stirring her responses until she could scarcely breathe, scarcely stand.

Instinctively she reached up her arms, wrapping them tightly around his neck, clinging to him in fevered desperation, as his hands slid down the length of her spine, curving her so intimately close against him that she could feel every warning tremor of male arousal as it shuddered through his hard-muscled body.

Her head fell back as she dragged dizzily for breath, and his kisses dusted scorching flames over her trembling eyelids, the wild pulse that fluttered beneath her temple; the hot tip of his tongue swirled into the delicate shell of her ear, sending shivers of heat through her veins.

With an impatient growl he reached for the belt of her raincoat. 'What have you got this thing on for?' he demanded.

'I didn't have a dressing-grown...'

With a deft movement he had unfastened it, murmuring with satisfaction as he slid his hands inside to find that beneath it she wore only a silky scrap of nightgown that reached barely a few inches down her thighs. She knew she ought to be stopping him, before it was too late, but as he gathered her up in a possessive embrace she felt the rasp of his hair-roughened chest against her breasts through the flimsy silk, a delicious reminder of her own feminine vulnerability, and the temptation to let herself surrender was almost overpowering.

His hand moved to cup one ripe breast, weighing its fullness in his palm as the pad of his thumb teased the tender nipple into a deliciously sensitised awareness. She heard her own voice, whimpering softly, pleading with an inarticulate urgency for him to satisfy the desperate longings that were tearing her apart.

Her spine was melting, and she was barely conscious that he had eased her back against the kitchen table, laying her across it. She knew only that he had lifted her skimpy nightgown, finding that beneath it she wore only a tiny pair of white lace briefs. His hungry gaze swept over her slender nakedness, savouring the peach-smooth curve of her stomach, dimpled by her dainty navel, and the firm round swell of her breasts, invitingly tipped with rosebud pink.

'You're so beautiful,' he breathed raggedly, stroking his hands up over her warm, flushed skin. 'I've wanted you from the first moment I saw you.'

Wanted—like a thing he could own, and enjoy at his pleasure. Not to love, nor to marry—that wasn't her role. She was to be his mistress, kept in luxury no doubt, but purely there to satisfy his physical desires. But as his hands smoothed up over her silken skin to mould and caress her aching breasts, she felt the last vestiges of her resistance melting away.

His head bent over her body, tasting the sweetness of her skin with his hot mouth, tracing paths of fire over her aching breasts. What sort of wanton creature had she become, for goodness' sake, letting him make love to her here on the kitchen table—as his fiancée slept innocently upstairs, not knowing that she was being betrayed?

But she no longer cared what was right or wrong; she was lost in a world of exquisite pleasure, and as he took one ripe, succulent nipple into his mouth, nibbling at it and swirling it with his rasping tongue, suckling with a deep, hungry rhythm, she ceased to be able to even think.

He lifted his head only long enough to move to the other breast, subjecting that nipple to the same sweet torment. His hands were caressing the slender length of her thighs, and she was aware that he had slid down the lace briefs that were the last shred of defence she possessed. But as his hands stroked back up over her silken skin, seeking the most intimate caresses, she could only yield in trembling submissiveness.

His touch was magical, exploring with exquisite sensitivity into the delicate velvet folds to find the tiny seed-pearl of pleasure nestling within, arousing it to a sizzling response that shafted through her like an electric current, making her gasp in shock, her spine curling to arch her body invitingly beneath his.

He laughed softly, stroking her hair back from her face. 'I didn't mean it to be here, but I want you too much to wait any longer,' he breathed huskily. 'You're so very desirable, it's been all I can do to keep my hands off you—and I'm afraid it's much too late to stop now.'

She opened misted eyes to gaze up at him, loving him so much it hurt. Just this one time—that was all they could have; any more would just compound the guilt and shame until she was robbed of every last shred of her self-respect. But all the angels in heaven couldn't expect her to deny him now...

She had been ready for pain, but there was none; he had been so patient, so gentle, that her body could surrender quite naturally to the hard shaft of his manhood, accepting the powerful thrust of his penetration with ease. No more than a small sigh escaped her lips, and she closed her eyes, feeling the deep,

intense pleasure of knowing that she belonged totally
to him.

'Are you all right?' he asked in tender concern.

'Oh, yes...'

He began to move inside her, slowly at first, gently
letting her become accustomed to these magical new
sensations, but then thrusting deeper, grinding into
her to stretch her deliciously, until she was moaning
and sobbing, swept up in the ferocity of his desire like
a leaf in a storm, wildly buffeted, gasping for breath.
She was spiralling in a vortex of heat, spinning up to
dizzy heights, lost to everything but the sheer mindless
bliss that was flooding her body, until she felt herself
melting, dissolving away into a pool of liquid gold.

Normal senses returned slowly; she became aware of
the hard kitchen table beneath her back, and as Jon
lifted his weight from her she sat up awkwardly. His
mouth was quirked into a slightly crooked smile as
he ran his hand back through his hair, ruffling it in
a way that she found heartbreakingly attractive. He
looked like the cat who had got the cream; and he
had, she acknowledged with a sharp twinge of humiliation—a wife who would be the kind of asset he
required in his public life, and a compliant mistress
to warm his bed.

Except that she wouldn't be his mistress—she
couldn't. It was no longer because of any scruples
about having an affair with an engaged—or married—
man, or guilt about Barbara, that held her back. It
was the knowledge that he would be taking her with
nothing but lust in his heart; that was just too painful
to bear.

Her golden hair fell across her face as she kept her head bowed to avoid his eyes. Straightening her nightgown, she wrapped her raincoat around her body. Her white briefs were on the floor, and she bent to pick them up—that discarded scrap of white lace seemed almost to taunt her; he had tossed it aside so casually—as casually as he had taken his pleasure from her. The sharp sting of tears pricked her eyes, and she struggled to blink them back.

He put out his hand to tilt up her chin, forcing her to look up at him. 'What's wrong?' he queried, frowning.

'That was wrong,' she countered with agonised conviction.

He looked puzzled. 'Why?'

'Because you only wanted me,' she whispered, unable to control the tremor in her voice. 'And I want you to love me. But I don't think you know how.'

His blank incomprehension told her that she was right, and she turned away, Khan padding at her side, puzzled but loyal, as she walked from the kitchen and climbed the stairs to her bedroom, closing the door behind her.

She had hung up her raincoat, and left her lace briefs on the chair—it seemed a little late to put them on now—when there was a soft rap on the door. She caught her breath, her heart leaping into her throat. It could be Barbara—she could have heard noises from downstairs, and have come to demand an explanation; it could be Hugo. Or it could be Jon. And if it was . . . ?

There was a second rap, and Khan jumped off the bed, running to the door as if to open it himself.

Steeling herself, she walked across the room and turned the handle.

It was Jon. He stood in the doorway, leaning one wide shoulder against the jamb, and his eyes were like drowning pools as he looked down at her. 'I could learn,' he asserted, a husky note of pleading in his voice.

What more could she do? She had tried her best, but she had no more resistance left. Without a word, she stood aside and let him into the room.

He closed the door behind him, reaching for her—but then with a wry smile paused and opened the door again, indicating to Khan that his presence was superfluous. The dog shot him a look of liquid reproach from beneath his yellow fringe, but reluctantly slunk out and settled himself with a huffing sigh on the floor.

'That's better,' murmured Jon with grim satisfaction, closing the door again. 'There's one place I draw the line, and that's sharing a bed with that brainless mutt.'

'He always sleeps with me,' Lacey protested, feeling it necessary to defend her beloved pet. 'He keeps me company.'

'You don't need him to keep you company,' he pointed out, scooping her up in his arms. 'You've got me.'

The November night was chilly, but beneath the bedclothes it was snug and warm; they were generating their own central heating—flesh on naked flesh, exploring all the pleasures of each other's bodies. Lacey discovered to her delight that running her fingertips down the length of his spine could produce an electrifying response, and that when she touched his flat, dark nipples with playful fingertips—or better still, the flickering tip of her tongue—she could reduce that powerful body to a state of quivering helplessness.

She giggled, savouring this wonderful new awareness of her power over him, seeking other spots equally sensitive—and finding plenty of them. And where she was too shy to touch, he gently encouraged her, guiding her small hands and teaching her what to do, until her desire to give him pleasure overcame her inhibitions, and she wriggled down under the bedclothes, letting her instincts take over, her soft lips and swirling tongue arousing him to an almost explosive peak of tension.

But instead of taking his immediate satisfaction he drew her up into his arms and laid her back on the bed, his skilful hands and scalding kisses inflaming her responses until she was lost in a world of pure ecstasy, every inch of her skin glowing, her breasts ravaged and aching, the tender peaks taut and throbbing, deliciously sensitised to his every touch.

She was still guiltily aware that what they were doing wasn't right, that she shouldn't be allowing him into her bed while he was engaged to someone else. But she knew that she couldn't deny him; if he wanted her to be his mistress, then that was what she would be, for as long as he wanted her. And though she knew that all she was going to get out of it was a broken heart, she no longer cared. She had been made to belong to him, and her only satisfaction would be to give him pleasure.

Jon chuckled with sensuous laughter, smiling down at her as he cradled her in his arms. 'My little wanton innocent,' he teased her. 'You're so sweet and generous—I'm going to enjoy teaching you everything about making love.'

She lifted her eyes to search his, but she couldn't be sure that what she saw there was anything more than the reflection of her own desperate hopes. The only thing she knew for certain was that she loved him, and she couldn't hold back the words, whispering them with all the aching sincerity she felt, offering him her heart as well as her body.

'We'll talk tomorrow,' was all he said, covering her mouth with his, his languorous tongue plundering the sweet, defenceless depths as his hand slid down over the smooth curve of her stomach to part her thighs and explore between, finding at once that exquisite seed of pleasure and gently arousing it, stroking it with one lightly sensitive fingertip, sparking fire into her brain.

'Please,' she heard herself begging brokenly. 'I want you . . .' She was reaching for him, drawing him down to her, her body arching invitingly to meet his hard possession. 'Make love to me,' she whispered, her voice ragged with desperation.

'I will,' he assured her, his breath warm against her cheek. 'All night, and every night from now on. I don't think I'll ever be able to have enough of you . . .'

He took her with one deep, forceful thrust that made her gasp. And then for a long moment they both lay still, feeling him inside her, just savouring the incredible power of the moment. This was it; this was what could drive him to betray the promise of his engagement, what could make her ignore the voice of her own conscience. It was like an obsession.

And then he began to move, slowly at first, guiding her to match his rhythm; her supple body willingly obeyed his every command, moving with him, offering itself in sweet surrender to the full measure of his demand. The tension inside her was mounting fiercely, wild as fire, hot as lightning, shafting through her until there was nothing but pure pleasure, exploding through her and leaving her shattered and exhausted, to sleep at last nestled in his arms.

CHAPTER NINE

LACEY woke abruptly, not sure what had shattered her sleep. Beside her Jon hadn't stirred; she could feel the warmth of his body against hers, hear the soft, steady sound of his breathing.

So it hadn't been a dream, what had happened last night; nothing could be more real than that big, solid body, all muscle and hard bone beneath gleaming bronzed skin, lightly smattered with fine, dark, curling hair. And that lingering musky scent, so primordially male, reaching out to some deep, feminine core inside her, where instinct alone ruled.

With a small sigh of contentment she nestled against his back, closing her eyes. He had had his way, as she had known almost from the beginning he would. She was his mistress. She turned the word over in her mind, trying to make herself grow accustomed to it. From now on she belonged to him, her sole purpose in life to give him pleasure—for as long as he wanted her. And she knew that as long as she lived she would never love anyone else...

There it was again... A shot. There could be no mistaking it. But what on earth...? Suddenly she stiffened, a horrific thought cutting through her brain. Khan! Jon had put him outside last night—had he made his way back to the kitchen and somehow managed to get out through that broken door-panel? She had forgotten all about it...

A wave of guilt swamped through her. What if he had gone off chasing sheep? If she hadn't let herself be so distracted... Swiftly she slipped out of bed, and pulled on her clothes, careful not to wake Jon—she didn't feel able to face him at the moment. It was all her fault—he was engaged to Barbara, and she should never have let him into her bed, however powerful the temptation. If anything had happened to Khan as a consequence, she would never forgive herself.

She tiptoed from the room, closing the door quietly behind her. There was no sign of her dog in the passage. She crept downstairs, desperate hope warring with fear in her heart; if only she could open the kitchen door, and find him lying there by the range... But the kitchen door was already ajar, and so was the door into the passage beyond—and she was sure she had closed it behind her last night. She hurried through. The piece of wood she had wedged across the broken door-panel had been scrabbled away, and the panel itself broken through—and clinging to a splinter was a small tuft of soft yellow fur.

'Oh, Khan...!' Sharp tears stung her eyes as she thought of those warm, trusting brown eyes, that soft body cuddling up to her, the bounce of mischief as he skittered across the room with something he had snatched. The echo of that shot was still ringing in her brain—had that been a farmer's gun?

Which way had the sound come from? It was hard to tell. A glance at her watch told her that it was barely half-past six—far too early yet for the newsmen to have emerged from the comparative comfort of their cars. Letting herself silently out through the back door, she hurried across the yard and scrambled over the low wall into a ploughed field.

The morning air was hung with damp mist that screened off the middle-distance, and the ground underfoot was muddy. Guided purely by guesswork, she cut diagonally across the field, and pushed her way through a thorn hedge into the next one. Another tuft of fur, caught among the bushes, told her she was going the right way.

'Please—let him be all right,' she whispered, straining her eyes to peer through the mist, her ears alert for the sound of his eager panting as he ran home. Nothing. 'Khan! Come on, poppet, come here.' Nothing; just mist and silence.

It served her right; she had known she was doing wrong, sleeping with another woman's man. Why oh why had she let herself be tempted? She had known that she would have to pay—but she had expected it to be in aching loneliness and sleepless nights, and ever after a sense that nothing would ever be so good again. Not this; not her darling Khan. That was too bitter a punishment, even for what she had done.

Another hedge, another field. The mist was seeping into her clothes, damp and cold, and it was hard going labouring over the deep ploughed furrows, the heavy earth sticking to her shoes. Maybe she should have put her raincoat on—but that would have meant going back upstairs to the room where Jon was sleeping, and she really hadn't wanted to do that. And anyway, it probably wouldn't have done a great deal of good against this penetrating chill.

The ground seemed to be rising steadily, and it had begun to drizzle with rain, but she trudged on, haunted

by a vision of what she was so afraid she would find—
that warm, lively body lying still and cold beneath a
hedge, the eyes closed forever.

'I'm sorry, Khan. I should have taken better care
of you. But you know that I always loved you...'

Ancient walls of dark grey stone loomed up tall and
menacing out of the rain and mist. Scatton Law, the
place that Mrs Dinsdale had spoken of in such fearful
tones. She had read about it in the old guidebook she
had found on the bookshelves at the farmhouse; these
were the ruins of the medieval castle that had held
the whole wild, windswept valley in thrall long cen-
turies ago.

The ghostly legend told of a young servant girl, who
had fallen in love with the lord of the castle and been
seduced by him, only to be abandoned. In her heart-
broken despair she had thrown herself from the
highest battlements to her death—but her wraith still
haunted the night, crying out forlornly for her lost
love.

It had taken Lacey more than three hours to get
this far. Wearily she sat down on a stone, wiping the
back of her hand across her nose—she hadn't brought
a handkerchief. She had never felt so cold and damp
and miserable in her entire life. And hungry; what she
wouldn't give for a nice thick slice of Mrs Dinsdale's
stotty-cake right now, spread thick with butter and
home-made bramble jam, and washed down with a
cup of that powerful tea. Even thinking about it was
torture.

There had been no sign of Khan. She had called
and called until her throat was sore and her voice was

no more than a croak, but there hadn't been an answering sound. He might not even have come this way—it could be deceptive, trying to judge the direction of a noise in this kind of open landscape, and the shots had been so brief. He could have gone in completely the opposite direction—he could be anywhere.

She leaned back against the wall behind her, and closed her eyes, not even trying to squeeze back the tears that trickled down her cheeks. All this exhausting walk, and maybe all for nothing. She might never find him, never know for sure what had happened to him.

And now she had to face the long walk back alone to the house—if she could even remember which way it lay. She had rather lost her bearings in the mist— she thought it must be over there to her right a little, but she couldn't be sure. But first she needed to rest a little—she was so tired. Colours swirled in her mind, fever-bright, and she slumped down the wall, sliding into a deep and dangerous sleep...

Khan was licking her face, and she tried weakly to push him off. Voices echoed around her head ... 'I've found her—over here.'

She tried to open her eyes, but she was so tired; it was so much easier just to go on sleeping. Someone had picked her up and was carrying her, and she let her head rest contentedly against his shoulder; she knew by the scent of his skin that it was Jon, but she could make no sense of what was going on, and her brain was too weary even to try...

*   *   *

The fire was glowing in the grate, casting dancing shadows over the walls. Something moved on the bed, and a wet, sloppy tongue licked her hand. 'Khan! Oh, Khan, you're safe! I thought you'd been shot.'

'So you're awake at last.'

She turned quickly, to see Jon sitting in the armchair beside the bed. He smiled down at her, moving across to sit on the edge of the bed, one gentle hand stroking a wayward strand of golden hair back from her face.

'How are you feeling?' he enquired.

'Not too bad,' she responded with some surprise, the memory of what had happened coming back to her. 'I'd...gone out to look for Khan. I heard a shot— it woke me up—and I found he wasn't in the house. He must have got out through the door into the stable-block. I was afraid he'd gone worrying sheep, and been caught by a farmer.'

'Damned mutt!' Jon castigated the chastened hound, now creeping up the bed to lie in the crook of Lacey's arm. 'If he hadn't turned out to have enough spark of intelligence to help us track you, I think I'd have wrung his stupid neck! While you were out hunting for him and damned nearly catching your death of cold, he was warm and cosy in Mrs Dinsdale's caravan.'

'Was he?' Lacey gurgled with laughter, hugging her beloved pet in relief. 'Oh, you *naughty* boy! I was so worried about you. What do you think the shots were that I heard, then?' she enquired, looking up at Jon.

He shrugged. 'Maybe someone trying to pot a rabbit. It could even have come from the army shooting range out on the moors.'

'Oh—I never even thought of that.' She yawned, and stretched luxuriously—and then with a sudden guilty start realised that it was Jon's bed she was in. She sat up quickly, her eyes flying to the door as if she expected an outraged fiancée to storm in, demanding to know what she was doing there.

Jon chuckled with laughter, guessing at once what was going through her mind. 'Relax,' he coaxed softly. 'Barbara's gone.'

'Gone?' She stared up at him in bewilderment.

'With your brother.'

Her eyes widened in shock. 'With *Hugo*? But... She can't possibly... He wouldn't... I don't understand.'

One dark eyebrow quirked in amused enquiry. 'I thought you'd guessed what was going on?' he teased.

'Yes, but...'

'While I was in your bed, he was in hers.'

She glared up at him in indignant fury. 'And you don't even *mind*? But she's your fiancée!' She tilted up her chin, turning her head away from him. 'I'm sorry, but I'm afraid I just can't understand that sort of relationship, and I'd rather not have anything to do with it, thank you.'

'Oh, Lacey, Lacey—you're so delightful when you're being cross,' he chuckled. Like a conjurer he produced something from his pocket—and Lacey was startled to see that large, square emerald ring lying in the palm of his hand. 'Our engagement has been little more than a polite fiction these past eighteen months, although it's suited us both, for various reasons, to maintain it. But we both knew we had to end the farce—and Hugo has very conveniently provided her with a way to avoid losing face.'

Lacey slanted him a suspicious glance from beneath her lashes. 'You never told me,' she accused. 'In fact you deliberately made me think you had every intention of marrying her.'

'Yes,' he confessed with a wry smile. 'I'm afraid that was a defensive tactic on my part. I knew I was getting very quickly out of my depth with you, and I was wary. You were something quite new in my experience—someone so generous and honest...'

'You didn't think I was honest the first time you met me,' she reminded him with a touch of asperity. 'You thought I was a tart.'

He laughed softly, shaking his head. 'Not really. Oh, you played the role very well—if I'd only seen you up on a stage, I'd have been utterly convinced. But your eyes were telling me something quite different—although it took me a little while to be sure that it wasn't just a case of being blinded by lust. And then, just when I was sure, I thought I'd lost you...' His voice wavered slightly, and he drew her into his arms, bending his head to bury his face in the softness of her hair. 'When I woke up and found you'd disappeared, I didn't know what to think—I had no idea where you'd gone. It wasn't until a couple of hours later, when Mrs Dinsdale came in with Khan, that we were able to put two and two together, and start looking for you.'

Lacey pulled a wry face. 'I'm sorry—I didn't mean to cause so much fuss,' she murmured.

'I know. You made the front pages again, though.'

He reached over to a table behind him, and handed her a newspaper. On the front page there was a photograph of him carrying her down from Scatton Law; it gave her an odd little feeling of pleasure to see herself in his arms like that—she would have to tear that picture out discreetly and keep it.

'They all joined in the hunt for you,' he told her, a glint of amusement lighting his eyes. 'The least I could do was let them have their pictures.'

'Ah, well—at least I look a little more decent in this one,' she chuckled. And then a sudden thought struck her, and she sought quickly for the date at the top of the page. 'But... This is Friday's paper,' she exclaimed in surprise.

Jon nodded. 'You've slept round the clock—more than round the clock, in fact—it's almost six in the evening.'

Lacey smiled. 'Well, if I've been asleep that long, no wonder I'm so thirsty. I could really do with...'

'A cup of tea?' he guessed shrewdly. 'Your wish is my command. Then try to sleep some more—we've quite an early start in the morning.'

'Why?' she asked, gazing up at him curiously. 'Where are we going?'

'Home.'

If Khan had felt that the leather-upholstered seat of an Aston Martin Vantage was an appropriate setting for his aristocratic mien, a priceless antique Chinese silk rug was even better. He was lounging luxuriously, his big front paws at full stretch, a small crumb of the chocolate biscuit he had inveigled out of Jon's mother still clinging to a corner of his contentedly smiling mouth.

Lacey couldn't feel quite so relaxed in these elegant surroundings. Oh, Jon's mother was very nice, and not at all intimidating; and though she still retained a good measure of what must once have been a quite striking beauty, it was clear that her looks weren't her top priority—the fine lines in her skin, and the signs of work on her hands, bore testament to a life spent out of doors tending her precious garden. And she hadn't turned a hair at having introduced to her the woman who had been named less than a week ago as her husband's mistress, and was now apparently her son's.

Clive, however, looked even more uncomfortable than she felt, perched in a large armchair, his fist clamped around a glass of brandy, as Jon and his lawyer worked out a form of words to explain to the newspapers the reasons for the 'misunderstanding' over the blackmail claim.

'I don't like it,' he objected petulantly. 'You're making me sound like a confounded old dodderer!'

'Shut up, Clive,' his wife advised him with crisp contempt. 'You're extremely lucky to be getting off so lightly.'

He lapsed into a sulky silence, voicing no further objections as his stepson calmly instructed him to sign the statement the lawyer had written out.

'Good.' Jon examined the signature, and laid the paper down on the table. 'The next point is your resignation from office.'

An expression of pain crossed the older man's bibulous countenance. 'No! Not that!'

'There's no other course of action open to you,' Jon pointed out coolly. 'When the PM hears about this he won't want to risk his own reputation by standing by you.'

For a moment Clive looked as if he might argue, but he knew he had no option. 'Damn you!' he muttered. 'Do whatever you like.'

Jon nodded grimly—he would have done anyway. Lacey felt a little nervous of him when he was in this mood—even though he was on her side. But she couldn't really feel sorry for Clive; he had brought this all on himself, and it certainly wouldn't be right for him to carry on being so close to running the country when he had been proved to be so duplicitous.

She slanted a covert glance across at Lady Fielding. She seemed to have taken the whole thing remarkably well; it was clear that she didn't hold her husband in very high regard—Lacey could well imagine that over the years his behaviour had strained her tolerance to breaking point. She certainly bore no resemblance to the somewhat downtrodden woman of her imagination—if anything, she seemed to be deriving a certain amusement from the present situation.

The lawyer—a slim, clever-looking young man with prematurely receding fair hair—was carefully transcribing a letter of resignation on Clive's behalf, which referred to his own and his wife's state of health, and expressing his thanks to his friend the Prime Minister, and to his constituency party, for their loyalty and support over the years of his 'very enjoyable political career'.

Clive signed it with a scowl, and sat back in his chair. 'There. Are you satisfied now?' he demanded belligerently.

'Just one more small point,' Jon responded evenly. 'The matter of the out-of-court settlement for the libel action Lacey is bringing against you.'

Lacey sat up sharply. 'What? But...I'm not bringing any libel action!' she protested.

'Yes, you are,' Jon informed her in a voice that would brook no opposition. 'Your lawyers have already been in contact with the lawyers for the *Beacon*.'

'My lawyers?' she repeated, puzzled.

'Me,' the fair-haired young man told her with a smile. 'Unless of course you would prefer to instruct someone of your own choosing?'

'No, of course not,' she demurred vaguely. 'I just... I don't know...'

'You don't want to let them get away with printing those kind of lies about you, do you?' Jon prompted her. 'You're entitled to have your good name fully restored.'

'Well, yes, but...'

'Sue them,' Lady Fielding advised briskly. 'They're far too ready to print any kind of nasty gossip. It'll serve 'em right.'

'Yes, but...' She looked at Lady Fielding, and the lawyer, and Jon, and finally shrugged her shoulders. 'All right,' she conceded. 'If you think I should...'

'Good.' Jon stood up, and took her hand, drawing her to her feet. 'Simon, I think we'll leave it to you to negotiate the details. I'd like to show Lacey the garden. Mother, you will stay to tea?'

'Of course, dear,' Lady Fielding responded, putting up her cheek for his kiss. 'I'll see you later—and you, dear,' she added kindly to Lacey.

Lacey managed some kind of uncertain response, and allowed Jon to lead her out through the French windows on to the terrace.

The house was in Roehampton, close to Richmond Park, but the garden could have belonged to a country estate. Tall trees lent it a quiet seclusion, and green paths winding between banks of flowering and ever-green shrubs opened charming vistas at every turn. Even in the pale sunlight of winter, it was still beautiful.

Jon slid his arm around her shoulders. 'Not too cold?'

She shook her head. 'It's a lovely garden,' she remarked, trying not to wonder too much what sort of discussions were taking place in the ivy-covered house behind them. 'Is your mother's garden like this?'

He shook his head. 'Bigger. And she goes in a lot for roses—old-fashioned shrub roses. They have a wonderful scent, and the most delicate colours. You'll love it.'

Lacey bit her lip, not at all sure that it was appropriate for him to assume in that casual way that his mother would be happy to entertain his mistress. But she really wasn't at all sure of the rules in this kind of society; it was all so unfamiliar. Even the tea was Earl Grey.

Another thought suddenly struck her, and she gurgled with laughter. Jon glanced down at her, quirking one dark eyebrow in amused question. 'I was just thinking about Barbara,' she explained. 'I still can't quite believe it—her and Hugo...!'

'I think she was a little taken aback by it herself,' Jon remarked. 'It does seem a little incongruous to think of her playing the groupie to a male stripper!'

Lacey's eyes danced. 'I wonder what she thought of the show last night?'

Jon began to laugh, and then laughed harder. 'I was going to say it would have been quite a revelation for her, but then I remembered—she'd already had a preview!'

She slanted a searching glance up at his face. 'Do you really...not mind?' she asked a little uncertainly.

He shook his head. 'To be honest, I would never have expected her to fall for a macho type like your brother, but she was looking very happy on it when I saw them off yesterday afternoon. I think he could be very good for her. And you never know... He's only five years younger than she is, and he's got rather more to him than a pair of well-developed biceps— she could even end up being your sister-in-law one of these days.'

'But...you must have been in love with her once,' she persisted wistfully.

He smiled down at her in wry self-mockery. 'I'm sorry to have to admit to you that I probably never was,' he responded. 'She was simply the sort of wife I'd always expected to have; from the right sort of background, with the right sort of education and accomplishments—a social asset. I had no reason to suppose I should look for anything different from the kind of marriage my parents had had—it had always seemed to meet their needs. But after we'd got engaged ... I don't know, somehow something always seemed to hold me back. I think Barbara guessed it quite early on, but it suited her to have me as a fiancé, even if she went out with other men. And I wasn't sufficiently bothered about it to make the break. I think I must have sensed I was waiting for something else all along.'

'Waiting for what?' she asked, her voice a little unsteady as she risked a look into those deep, dark, hypnotic eyes.

'Something very precious,' he murmured, his voice taking on a husky timbre as he stopped walking and drew her into his arms. 'A woman who knows what love really is, who could show me what it means to care.'

His lips brushed over hers, light as a butterfly's wings, and she felt herself melting, all her dreams flowing together into this one sweet moment. She lifted her arms to wrap them tightly around his neck, kissing him back with all the vibrant love in her heart.

He lifted his head, his dark eyes gazing down into hers. 'I think I'm going to have to become a perpetual student of the subject,' he murmured teasingly. 'In which case, there's only one thing to do—I shall have to marry the teacher.'

Lacey's violet-blue eyes widened in astonishment, but she knew from the tenderness in his smile that he meant it. 'I ... Yes!' she breathed, her heart spilling over. 'Oh, yes, please!'

He picked her up and swung her round, laughing for joy. 'We'll get married right away,' he insisted. 'And I'll whisk you off for the most romantic honeymoon in the world.'

'I've already had a honeymoon,' she reminded him shyly. 'And if I'm going to have another one, I'd like to have it in the same place.'

The way his eyes lit up told her that he was of the same mind. 'There's just one thing,' he temporised warily. 'Do we have to take...?'

At that moment a spring-loaded bundle of yellow fur hurtled around the corner, and launched himself against them, barking excitedly, as if he hadn't seen them for weeks. Lacey laughed, and hugged the exuberant pup, gazing up pleadingly at Jon.

With a sigh of laughing resignation, he shrugged his wide shoulders. 'Oh, all right,' he conceded. 'But he's not sleeping on the bed!'

HARLEQUIN ◆ PRESENTS®

Follow your heart, not your head,
in our exciting series:

—when passion knows no reason...

Watch for these dramatic stories about women who
know the odds are against them—
but take the risk all the same!

Dare to love in:

June 1997—HIS COUSIN'S WIFE (#1891)
by Lynsey Stevens
July 1997—WHISPER OF SCANDAL (#1898)
by Kathryn Ross

Available wherever Harlequin books are sold.

HARLEQUIN ✦ PRESENTS®

Three women make a pact to stay single...
But one by one they catch

and then the magic begins!

Don't miss this compelling new trilogy
from bestselling author

PENNY JORDAN

Take a trip to the altar in:

June 1997—BEST MAN TO WED? (#1889)
July 1997—TOO WISE TO WED? (#1895)

Available wherever Harlequin books are sold.

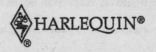